Inside the Masidone Mansion

Inside

the

Masidone

Mansion

Brandy Blackmon

ISBN: 979-8-9928220-0-7

Cover Design by Sandra Rzeczya
Interior Design by Brandy Blackmon

This is a work of fiction. Names, characters, places, and incidents are products of the author's imagination or used fictitiously. Any resemblance to actual events, locales, or people, living or dead, is entirely coincidental.

First Edition: April 2025
Printed in the United States of America
For permission or inquiries, contact:
Brandy Blackmon at: blackmonbrandy27@gmail.com

Inside the Masidone Mansion

From the *Choices* series

Other books currently in this series:

My Choice

From the Choices We made

To those that may feel alone or trapped.
You aren't, even if you don't realize it.
Lean on those that you love and that love you.

Chapter 1

It almost felt like a dream to be away from home. The occasion was rare—at least, being away without our dad. I had to take it all in, every minute of it. Rolling down my window, I inhaled deeply, savoring the fresh, non-mansion air. I couldn't even remember the last time we'd managed to sneak away from his supervision.

"Are you sure this is where you want to go? You know Papa Masy doesn't like us going places he's never been. How did you even find this spot?" Jay asked, eyeing the entrance to the outdoor mall through the windshield. The way he was acting, you'd think we had him drive us somewhere illegal.

I seemed to be the only one excited about spending the day out. Sure, sneaking two hours away from home without Dad knowing was risky, but Jay could never resist an adventure. He knew what could happen, yet here we were anyway. If we got in trouble, we all got in trouble.

"Don't you remember? We passed by here on our way home about a month ago," I reminded him. "The place looked interesting, so I wanted to check it out. Weren't you curious too?" I turned to Sano.

"Yeah, I remember." He glanced out the window. "Mom and Dad definitely wouldn't find us here. I'm sure we won't stand out too much—just look at all these people." His words dripped with sarcasm.

I followed his gaze and immediately saw what he meant. Even from inside the car, I could tell we looked different. The people here wore baggy clothes, had messy hair, and—was that a fake designer bag? Mom owned two from that brand, and I knew for a fact the logo didn't look like that.

Dad would never let us go somewhere this public. If he found out, we'd be heading straight home. Jay always let us have fun, though. Even though he was worried, he knew that if it were up to him, we'd never get to visit places like this.

"Alright, you two," Jay said as we stepped out. "We have forty-five minutes to look around before we need to head back. If Papa Masy gets home before us, you can kiss these little adventures goodbye."

I didn't see what was so bad about this place—it was just a mall. But Sano was right—we did stand out in our brand-new, multicolored designer polo shirts from last week. It was probably obvious we had money. Dad always said he wanted the best for us, so every month, we got piles of new stuff. I could never bring myself to tell him it was too much. I didn't see the big deal in keeping up with the latest trends.

"Hey, Ken, check this out." Sano tapped my arm and pointed to a store where a guy was riding some kind of board.

"Oh, I think I've seen those on TV before. It's like a Segway without the handles," I said as we moved closer.

"Interested in a hoverboard?" the sales guy asked, gliding toward us while still balancing on the board. I'd seen these in ads all the time—he barely moved his body, yet he zipped around effortlessly.

"I bet you couldn't ride that," Sano joked.

"I'd ride it way better than you could," I shot back.

"It's simple, really. Just lean in slightly, and it moves forward. Same with going backward. Apply a little more pressure to each foot to turn," the sales guy explained, demonstrating as he moved. The more he showed off, the more I wanted one.

"I'm pretty sure a friend of mine has one," Jay said from behind us. "But I don't know if you boys could handle it, seeing as you couldn't even handle skating." He laughed, recalling the time Sano and I raced in the backyard. We hadn't noticed something on the ground and went crashing while trying to dodge it.

"That was a one-time accident," I said defensively.

"Wouldn't have happened if you didn't crash into me," Sano added.

"We could redo that race with one of these."

"Do you really think Papa Masy would let you get this?" Jay asked.

"If we could have skates, we can get one of these. He'd be fine. And if not, Mom definitely would be," I assured him. She was way more open-minded than Dad. He probably wouldn't want us getting one, but if we showed Mom first, she might be able to change his mind.

"I still don't think you could ride it without falling on your face," Sano laughed.

"If you're really interested in buying one, I might let you take a test ride," the sales guy offered, stepping off the board.

"I'll give it a shot," I volunteered.

"You sure you don't need a helmet?" Sano smirked.

"Now, don't be like that," Jay snickered. "He might need more than a helmet. Maybe a crash mat as well?" He joined in on the teasing. Even the sales guy looked like he was holding back a laugh.

"It's not that hard. I'll guide you. If you can stand on it, you'll already be doing better than most," the guy said, positioning himself in front of the board.

I stepped up behind it and studied it for a second. If moving one foot made it turn, I'd probably have to get on quickly. I noticed that when he got off, he barely moved his feet, so the board didn't roll away. The best way to get on was to step straight onto it.

The thought of falling and breaking everything in the store crossed my mind, but I wasn't about to let them have the satisfaction of thinking

7

I couldn't do it. Carefully, I stepped on. The board shifted forward slightly, but I didn't fall. Leaning forward like he said, I started moving.

"Aren't you a natural!" the sales guy said.

"You two were saying?" I tried turning to face them. Another victory for me.

"I call beginner's luck," Sano scoffed.

"So you can dance around on your little moving platform. I still don't know how Papa Masy is going to react to seeing these in the house."

"Then he just won't see them," I said, hopping off. "It's not like we're bringing home a car."

"Alright, fine. Just don't come looking for me if something happens," Jay said, giving in. It never took much to get him to come around.

"Sounds like you'll be getting one?" the sales guy asked.

"Make that two," Sano added. "You're not having all the fun. We'll see who falls first."

"I can see you two get along well," the guy laughed. We were brothers—of course we got along.

We bought our hoverboards and checked out. The guy looked surprised when Sano and I paid for ourselves. One of the good things about being this far from home—no one knew who we were. He had no idea we were part of the Masidone family, and I was glad for that. Once people figured it out, they started acting overly nice, hoping to get money out of us. We already gave to a lot of charities, so the extra handouts became a bother sometimes.

"If you boys are done here, why not keep looking around? Remember, we're on a tight schedule," Jay reminded us.

We left the store and kept walking. I recognized some of the store names from past trips to the mall with Mom, but there were plenty I'd never heard of. If we had more time, I would've explored every single one, just to see what they had. Something told me we wouldn't be coming back here often.

"Ken, I see another store we should check out." Sano nudged me and pointed toward a jewelry store. I looked up and didn't recognize the name, but as I followed his gaze, I realized he wasn't just interested in the store. His eyes were locked on two girls standing by a display, pointing at something and laughing.

"What are you two—"

"Hold on, Jay," Sano cut him off.

Jay followed our line of sight and finally noticed the two girls. They were chatting and giggling about something, clearly entertained. I had no idea why Sano suddenly stopped to watch them, but now I was curious about what was so funny.

They looked like regular girls, about our age. Thanks to Jay's 'Designer 101' lessons, it was easy to tell they weren't all that into high-end fashion. But from the way they carried themselves, it didn't seem like that kind of thing mattered to them.

"Really now? Is this what you two wanted by coming here?" Jay questioned.

"We just wanted to get out, is all," I replied. "We just happened to notice others doing the same thing."

"Oh, really now?" His skepticism was obvious.

I was about to look away when one of the girls reached into her bag. She rummaged around for a moment, then suddenly froze. Her happy expression vanished, replaced by something close to panic. She looked like she was on the verge of crying.

"Aw, did she forget something? The poor thing," Jay mused. Then he turned to us with a smirk. "Now, boys, seeing as you're almost teenagers—well, Kenny-kens anyway," he clarified, "my grown man Sano here has already made the crossover—you're going to have to learn how to handle a woman when she cries. Remember, treat her with care. Try to understand what led to the tears and act accordingly. I won't allow you young Masidone boys to be the reason a girl cries, you hear me?" Jay was giving us Girl 101.

He knew something about everything. I figured his years in theater had forced him to learn a bit about different people and personalities.

I glanced back at the store. For some reason, I couldn't shake the feeling that something was going on. When I looked over at Sano, he was already staring at me, thinking the exact same thing.

"I suddenly feel like checking out this store," I said, my curiosity growing.

"Me too," Sano added.

"Listen here, you lady killers," Jay warned. "Papa Masy would have my head served fresh on a gold platter if I let you go girl shopping when we're not even supposed to be shopping."

"There won't be any serving if he doesn't know what's on the menu, right?" I shot him a look, repeating something I'd overheard him say on the phone the other day.

Jay sighed. "I thought I heard you outside my room that day. Kelly's going to give me an earful for that comment." He pointed a finger at us. "You two better not do anything that'll have her coming for me!"

"Thanks, Jay! You know Mom could never be mad at you. You're like another son to her. We won't do anything bad—we swear."

Sano and I headed toward the store. Jay always had our backs. He was Mom's favorite nephew, which meant if Dad found out about anything, she'd defend us—and bail him out too.

We stepped inside, passing a shelf lined with sunglasses. Jay had a huge collection, but I didn't recognize any of these brands. Some of them were priced ridiculously high. I wouldn't have expected girls like them to shop at a place like this.

10

I glanced over. The two girls were still standing near a rack marked clearance. Honestly, I wasn't even sure why we'd come in. The closer we got, the less of a plan I had for what to do next.

"So, do you want to talk to them?" Sano whispered.

I picked up a pair of dark blue sunglasses, similar to the ones Jay had hanging from his matching black-and-blue-trimmed shirt. I put them back down and stole another glance at the girls.

"Ugh, why must I be so poor?! I thought I had enough for this," one of them groaned.

"It's okay, we can wait a little longer," the other reassured her.

"But we said we'd get them this week. We keep waiting because I didn't have the money."

The girl who had looked like she was about to cry sounded frustrated—like money was something she struggled with a lot.

I had never in my life wanted something and not been able to get it because of money. The thought of saving up for something and still not having enough… That must be hard.

"I'll go over there if you don't," Sano smirked.

I hadn't expected him to be so eager to talk to girls. He was usually pretty closed off. Maybe it was a teenager thing to start having an interest in them. And now he was looking at me like I was supposed to go talk to them instead. Normally, I wouldn't care either way in situations like this. Talking to people wasn't a big deal. But for some reason, I hesitated.

"It's okay. Just get it another time. It's no big deal. We still have a little time," the other girl said.

Sano shot me a look—daring me.

"But—"

"Pardon the intrusion," I said suddenly, stepping forward. "I couldn't help but overhear your money shortage."

"What's it to you?" The girl who had been trying to comfort her friend took a step forward, her tone sharp. She didn't seem as friendly as I'd thought...

"Well, I happen to have some extra money, and I'm willing to help you out."

"No! I don't need someone else's help!" the sad one blurted. She put down what she was holding but didn't let go completely. It was obvious she really wanted it, but for some reason, she refused to accept my offer.

She was different from the girls I knew. They wouldn't hesitate to say yes when offered something.

"It looks like you really want that," I said. "I just wanted to offer some help."

"It's okay, she said no, so it's fine," the other girl cut in.

"Wait!" The first girl started again. "Katie, you know I have that trip next week. If I don't do this now, I really won't be able to. And we promised forever ago that we'd get these bracelets. These are the only ones left. What if they don't restock? I mean, they are on clearance."

She hesitated, then turned to me.

"If you're really offering, that would be awesome. It's not much anyway—just a few bucks." She started counting her money again.

I glanced at what she was so eager to buy—two silver-plated charm bracelets with a heart split down the middle. One side had 'best,' and the other side had 'friends'. When put together, they formed a whole.

They must be really close for her to want this so badly.

"I wouldn't even notice that was gone," I told her.

She grabbed the bracelets, and we headed to the counter. I glanced back and saw Sano still by the sunglasses, watching.

"There you go, dear," the cashier said after we paid, handing her the bag.

12

She took it with the biggest smile. I'd never seen someone look so happy over something so small.

As we walked toward the exit, she suddenly stopped and turned to me.

"Thank you for the help. If I could, I'd pay you back."

She wouldn't meet my eyes, like she was embarrassed to say it. She shifted on her feet, hesitating—like there was something else she wanted to say.

"Do you live around here? If we go to the same school, I could pay you back later!" she asked, eyes filled with hope. She really seemed to want to make it up to me.

Handing out money wasn't exactly how I saw this adventure going, but then again, I hadn't expected to be talking to girls either.

"Something that small isn't worth worrying about," I shrugged. I didn't want to tell her I wasn't from the area, that the chances of us running into each other again were practically nonexistent.

The hopeful look on her face faded. She looked disappointed, and for a brief second, I almost wanted to lie—say I was from around here. But before I could say anything, she turned back to her friend.

"W-well, Katie, I'm sorry this took so long, but here they are—our official best friend bracelets. These should last way longer than those cheap ones that turned our arms green." She pulled one from the box and fastened it around her friend's wrist. I almost felt like I was watching a marriage proposal.

"And this one's yours," Katie said with a smile. "You truly are a good friend, Misa. I'll cherish it always."

They stood side by side, pressing their wrists together so the broken heart charms formed a whole.

"You better," I said, smirking. "It's not every day I help out the poor."

The lighthearted moment shattered instantly.

Katie's head snapped toward me, her expression twisting in anger. "Help out the what?"

I blinked. "You said it earlier, right? You called yourself poor and said you didn't have much money. Am I wrong?"

"Wrong or not, how can you just look down on us like that?! What makes you so special?" She stepped toward me, fists clenched.

"Katie, don't!" Misa pulled her back. Her voice trembled as she added, "He... he's right, though. I don't have a lot of money right now. So yeah, I am kind of poor. That's just how it is."

Her face turned red, tears welling in her eyes. Then, without another word, she spun around and hurried off. She didn't make it far. With a sharp gasp, she tripped over a bench and hit the ground hard.

Katie instinctively took a step forward but hesitated, her hands shaking. Then, instead of rushing to Misa, she turned back to me. "People like you are the worst!"

Before I could react, her palm smacked across my face so hard that I stumbled back, grabbing onto a railing to keep from falling. By the time I recovered, Katie was already running to help Misa. The two of them walked away, leaving me standing there, still trying to process what just happened.

Footsteps pounded toward me.

"Sweet heavens, are you okay?!" Jay skidded to a stop in front of me, eyes wide. "I was watching, but I couldn't hear what was going on! Why on earth did she slap you?"

"Because Ken is an idiot," Sano said, finally stepping out of the store.

Jay sighed, rubbing his temples. "Idiot or not, how am I supposed to explain this to Papa Masy?" He pulled out his phone and started dialing.

"Chris, I need you to follow someone. Leave the car to me," he said to our driver.

14

I frowned. "Are you really sure that's necessary?"

Jay's gaze flicked to my face. "You were assaulted. I need to know who they were. Look at you—I didn't know you could turn that red."

I instinctively touched my cheek. It still stung. That girl had power.

Sano shook his head like he was personally offended. "Here's a tip—don't tell a girl she has nothing while handing her a pity handout."

"Oh, like you would've handled it any better."

"Yeah, I would have," he shot back without hesitation. "But you're still a kid. You've got a lot of growing up to do. We'll have to fix that so you don't blow it next time." He patted my shoulder, laughing.

I turned, glancing in the direction they had gone. They were already out of sight. Should there even be a next time?

"Our little adventure is officially over," Jay announced. "I'm taking you boys home. We need to get your face checked out."

"The worst I'll get is a little bruise. I'll be fine," I muttered. Jay always worried more than my own mom when I got hurt.

"That girl was rough," Sano mused. "I liked the calmer one."

"I don't like either of them," Jay said flatly. "For now, you stick to the people I know—people I have the authority to deal with if necessary."

It felt like we were listening to Dad right now.

Jay had only recently been appointed as our guardian when Mom and Dad weren't around, and he clearly wasn't looking to take any risks that could get him into real trouble.

As my face grew stiffer with every passing minute, I could only hope the long drive home was long—long enough for the redness to fade before anyone saw it.

Chapter 2

It took two days for my face to heal.

Dad took one look at me and immediately knew we'd left the house. Anger was an understatement. He stripped us of everything—our phones, our privileges, even our freedom to leave without an escort. He locked us down under his watch, confining us to the punishment room near his office, where he could keep us in sight at all times.

For nearly two weeks, our lives became a cycle of school, homework, and counting the tiles on the walls. If we were even a minute late coming home, Dad would call, demanding to know why.

Finally—after what felt like an eternity—we were freed from confinement and got our phones back. Not for our own use, but so Dad could check in with us directly. We still weren't allowed to go anywhere.

Sano and I spent most of our time in our room, strategizing ways to get Dad to ease up. Just as I was about to suggest apologizing for the twentieth time, a knock sounded at the door.

"I have good news!" Jay's voice rang out as he stepped inside.

Sano and I were huddled over his desk, mapping out our options. Jay took one look at us and smirked. "Whatever you two are plotting can wait—because I have something better." He held up a manila folder like it was a prized possession.

"What you got there, Jay?" Sano asked, eyes narrowing with interest.

Jay grinned. "Freshly gathered *evaluations* on our little assault demon." He threw up air quotes.

"Wait... you're not talking about those girls, are you?" I asked, half-expecting him to be joking. I hadn't thought he'd actually gone through with it—especially since it had been two weeks.

Jay tossed the folder onto the desk. Sano and I both reached for it at the same time.

"You actually had her followed," Sano muttered, more a realization than a question.

I was already flipping through the pages.

"Well," Jay said casually, "Kelly helped me smooth things over, but since I already had Chris on the job, I figured—why not see what he finds? That way, I'd know if there was anything actually worth reporting to Papa Masy or not."

I froze.

If Dad knew what really happened—that I got slapped by a girl instead of Sano playfully hitting me—there was no telling how he'd react.

"You don't have anything to report," I said, pointing to a name on the page a bit relieved. "Misa Macky. If I remember correctly, she wasn't the one who slapped me." I skimmed through more of the report.

"It was Katie," I said as I recalled that day. "She's the one who hit me."

"Yeah, I remember hearing that now," Sano added.

Jay groaned. "Are you serious? That Chris—I gave him one job." He shook his head in frustration.

"To be fair, he did do the job pretty well," I pointed out. "Just... on the wrong person."

Sano leaned in over my shoulder as I kept going. "Man, he dug up everything. Her school, where she lives... oh, look at this—she had an accident on a trip. Slipped down three flights of stairs and ended up in the hospital."

"Ouch. That had to hurt," Sano muttered.

"I'd assume so. Huh. Poor thing." Jay sighed and pulled out his phone. "Alright, I'll tell Chris to put a pin in this investigation."

"Now, hold on a minute." I held up a finger before he could dial.

Jay raised an eyebrow. "What now?"

"I was hit pretty hard, you know. Maybe I got them mixed up. Maybe this is actually who we want."

"What are you getting at?"

"I'm just saying… the least we can do is wait and see if Chris gets any updates on her condition." I shrugged. "Would be bad if you're still holding a grudge against her and she—" I gestured vaguely, "—suffered fatally."

"You want to keep surveilling her? What, did you fall in love or something?" Sano joked.

"Don't be ridiculous." I scoffed, but I hesitated. What am I doing?

I thought back to that day—the way her face lit up after buying those bracelets, how determined she was to pay me back. And then I went and insulted her. And now… she'd been in the hospital?

Jay sighed. "I should check on Papa Masy. He's already uneasy. If he heard you talking like this, he'd never let you out of the house again."

Dad always wanted us to act the way a proper, well-kept family should. But I never let him forget that Mom was nothing like that either, and yet, they were still together. I'd overheard them arguing about it a few times, but in the end, they always seemed fine.

"About time he opened up his options," I muttered.

"Yeah, well, not while he's in the middle of a big contract negotiation." Jay shot me a warning look. "He's under a lot of stress right now. Don't give him more to worry about."

He picked up the folder and tucked it under his arm. "I'll hold onto these for now—so you don't add this to whatever you two were plotting."

"Ken probably already has everything engraved in his memory anyway," Sano shrugged.

I didn't argue—because he wasn't wrong. Sometimes, I remembered more than I wanted to.

Sano leaned back in his chair, smirking. "That girl wanted to pay you back, right?" He stretched lazily, then threw me a knowing look. "Let's make a bet. If we ever see them again, whoever can talk to them the longest without getting slapped is the better man. And no talk of charity this time."

I narrowed my eyes. He was just as curious as I was.

"Alright, let's do it." We shook hands, sealing the deal.

Jay let out an exaggerated sigh. "My, my. You two are something else. I think it's about time Kelly had *the talk* with you." He turned and walked out.

"Speaking of Mom..." Sano's tone shifted, more serious now. "You don't think she's mad at us about something, do you?"

I frowned. "No. I mean, she wasn't thrilled about what happened, but she let that go a while ago. Did she say something to you?"

"That's just it. She hasn't said much the past few days. I tried talking to her yesterday, and she just looked... worried."

"You think she and Dad had another fight?"

"I don't know. I doubt it. Jay would've said something. I was thinking maybe I did something..."

"You always jump to that conclusion." I gave him a look. "You haven't done anything, have you?"

"No. At least, I don't think so..." He trailed off, still deep in thought.

"She probably just has something on her mind. You worry too much." I nudged him. "You always think you're in trouble when I'm usually the one causing problems."

That got a small smirk out of him, but the worry lingered.

Mom rarely got upset with us unless we did something really bad. And even then, she usually let it go.

We dropped the conversation and went to bed. Maybe the thought stayed on my mind as I felt uneasy all night. I barely slept. And when I saw Mom the next morning, it was worse.

She barely looked at me. Barely muttered a "good morning" before walking off.

Sano might've been right. Something was wrong. I'd never seen her like this before. And that made my stomach knot in a way that had nothing to do with hunger.

Classes that day passed in a blur—nothing out of the ordinary happened there. Even the extra homework didn't bother me. But the moment we got in the car to head home, that uneasy feeling crept back in.

When we stepped inside the house, it hit me like a gut punch.

Mom was walking out of Dad's office, that same troubled expression from this morning still etched on her face.

"Boys, you're home," she said, forcing a small smile. "I hope you had a good day at school." Then she hesitated, pressing her fingers against her wrist like she was checking her own pulse. "I suppose I can't keep putting this off. We need to sit down and have a talk."

I froze. Mom never said phrases like 'have a talk'. I glanced at Sano. He met my eyes with the same confusion, his brows furrowing.

"What's wrong?" I asked.

"Could you follow me to the dining room?" She didn't answer the question. Jay stood behind us, silent. When I turned to him, he just looked away. That uneasy feeling doubled. Without hesitation, we followed. Had Jay told her about having *the talk*?

Mom sat at the dining table, exhaling deeply. Her fingers twisted together in her lap.

"Ken, Sano…" She hesitated, voice low, serious—the tone she only used when something was really important. This wasn't about *the talk*. This was worse.

20

"Your father and I are having… troubles."

Sano sat up straighter. "What kind of troubles?"

Her throat bobbed as she swallowed. "Marital trouble. We've tried and tried, but it's becoming too much for us." she pause, taking a deeper breath. "We're getting a divorce." Her voice was barely above a whisper. Yet it hit like a freight train.

Her hands were clasped so tightly her knuckles had gone white. Silence filled the room. I stared at her, my mind scrambling to catch up. They fought sometimes, sure. But this? I never thought it was this serious.

"I'm so sorry I had to tell you like this," Mom continued. "Everything happened so fast, and I kept trying to find the right way to say it, but… there really isn't one." Her voice cracked, but she pressed on.

"I want you both to know this isn't because of you. You had absolutely nothing to do with it. Your father and I just aren't seeing eye to eye anymore, and we think it's best to separate." She hesitated before adding, softer this time, "And… I'll be leaving the house."

I stiffened. "You're leaving?"

"It would be difficult, given our situation, if I stayed. So yes, it's best that I leave…" She took a slow inhale, her fingers pressing into her own skin like she was holding herself together. "And you both will stay here with your father."

Sano's voice wavered. "So you don't want us with you?"

"No, no, honey, it's nothing like that." She reached across the table, taking his hand. "Don't ever think that. But I truly believe you'll both be better off here. This way, I know you'll have everything you need, and you'll be okay."

She glanced between us, her grip tightening. "You can visit me anytime you want. I'll give you all the details about where I'll be. And

21

Jayson will be here with you. He said that even though we aren't together anymore, he won't leave you two."

It was reassuring to know Jay wasn't leaving too since I know he isn't actually related to Dad. But this didn't make it hurt any less. I swallowed hard, my mind spinning. Mom was leaving... How am I supposed to take this?

"Is there anything you want to say?" she asked gently.

Of course, there was. That this was unfair. That we shouldn't have to live apart. That even though they were both gone a lot, I never thought one of them would never come back. But would saying that change anything? Would it make her stay?

"If this will make you happier, then I'm okay with it," Sano suddenly said, breaking the silence. Just yesterday, he had worried she was upset with him. There was no way he'd say something now that might actually upset her.

"Yeah, me too," I added. I didn't want her to go, but I didn't want to make her sad by asking her to stay.

She started tearing up as she looked at both of us. "You boys are growing up so much. I'm so sorry to do this to you," she said, her voice shaky.

A tug pulled at my chest. I had never seen her this sad before. I glanced at Sano. His expression was calm, but there was pain in his eyes. His body seemed stiff, as if he were holding back how he really felt. He didn't want her to go, but he also believed she shouldn't have to stay just for us. And besides, her mind seemed made up. I didn't think there was anything we could say to change it.

"I love you both so much. I hope you know that," she said, squeezing our hands.

"We'll be okay, Mom. You're leaving the house, but we'll still see you, right? Don't worry." I tried to reassure her. Tears welled in her eyes, spilling down her cheeks. Seeing Mom like this—I couldn't stand it.

Even though I hated this, putting on a brave face seemed like the best thing to do for her.

"Thank you for understanding. You two just got home. I'm sure you have other things you want to do today. I'll let you go. I'll still be here for a few more days while I pack my things, so please talk to me whenever you need me." She wiped her face before turning to Sano, then back to me.

"Oh, I almost forgot something important. Ken, could you give your brother and me a minute?"

"Uh, sure." Her sudden request to talk to Sano alone only confused me more, but I stood up slowly and left the room. As I stepped out, I noticed Jay leaning against the wall.

"I'm so sorry, Kenny-kens. She just told me today too."

"I can't say this makes me happy, but it doesn't seem like something we could have stopped. But now she's talking to Sano alone. She asked me to leave."

"She's talking to him now? Already?" Jay straightened.

"Yeah, right after she told us, she asked to speak with him privately. Do you know what it's about?" His expression of surprise told me he did.

"I don't have all the details yet. But if it's about what I found out a little while ago…" Jay trailed off.

A cold sweat formed on my skin, leaving me uneasy. We had just found out our parents were getting a divorce and Mom was leaving. What else could be so bad?

"I'm going in there with them. I'll talk to you later," Jay said, his voice unusually calm. That alone told me this was serious. I only nodded and headed to my room.

I always knew this family had secrets. And I had a feeling some of them weren't going to stay secret much longer…

23

Waiting for answers felt like hours, but according to the clock on the wall, it had barely been twenty minutes. Jay had gone in with them, leaving me alone to wait until they were done talking—talking about something that didn't include me. Could she really be upset with Sano about something else?

"Young Masidone?" A knock on my door was followed by a voice that caught me off guard. It sounded like one of the maids. "I have your laundry done. Where would you like me to put it?"

"Anywhere is fine," I told her, calming my nerves a bit when I realized that was all she wanted.

"I'll return with the rest in a moment," she said. The door was almost shut when it suddenly stopped and reopened.

"I just left you both some laundry. I will return with the rest."

I looked over and saw she was speaking to Sano. He stepped inside, and she closed the door behind him.

"So, what happened?" I didn't hesitate to ask.

"I... don't really know."

"What do you mean you don't know? What were you two talking about all this time?"

"She was about to tell me something, but then Jay walked in. They started talking for a bit. Then she just gave me this." He held up a folded piece of paper and handed it to me. I opened it and read the name written on it.

"Sasha Sanders? Who's that?"

"Mom said she works part-time at a restaurant and also teaches Japanese at a school on the other side of town. She wants me to go see her."

"But why? Who is this person?"

"I don't know. She didn't say. Or rather, she wants me to meet her first before explaining anything." He took the paper back from my hand.

"Are you going to see her?"

24

"Should I? I've never heard of a Sasha Sanders before. But Mom gave me all her details—phone number, address, and where she works. So, they clearly know each other. That doesn't explain why I need to meet her, though."

"You want to call the number?"

"And say what? I don't even know who she is," he repeated.

"Just call and pretend you got the wrong number. At least that way, we can hear what she sounds like." My curiosity was growing rapidly.

Sano tightened his grip on the paper, his eyes narrowing as he debated what to do.

"I'll call if you want. I'll put it on speaker," I offered.

His tension eased slightly. I took the paper from his hand and dialed the number.

"It's ringing." I switched to speaker mode, waiting. Then, the call connected.

"Hello?" a woman's voice answered. Sure enough, I'd never heard it before.

"Uh, I-is this Sandy?" I asked. Sano raised an eyebrow, giving me a funny look. I shrugged, drawing a blank. Calling a random number wasn't exactly on my to-do list today.

"No, this is Sasha, not Sandy. Are you calling for Sasha?" she asked.

"Ah, no, sorry. I must have the wrong number."

"I see. Well, that happens sometimes," she laughed.

"Yeah, sorry about that. Goodbye."

"Bye now." We both ended the call.

"Well... she seems friendly," I said after that awkward conversation.

"Her voice sounds oddly familiar," Sano murmured, deep in thought.

"It does? So maybe you've met her before and just don't remember."

"Maybe…"

"Are you going to go see her? I'll go with you if you want."

"Jay said he'd take me himself if I decided to go. If you go, then I'll do it," he said, making up his mind.

"Okay, cool. Did Mom say where or when to meet her?"

"She said if I agreed, we should go after school tomorrow."

"Tomorrow? So soon?" I frowned. Mom had just told us she and Dad were divorcing, and now she suddenly wanted Sano to meet some lady? What was going on with her?

"This is all so strange. First, she tells us she and Dad are divorcing, and now I have to meet someone I don't even know," Sano said, echoing my thoughts.

"Think it has something to do with the divorce?"

"Why would it?"

"It didn't come up until now, right? She could've mentioned it any other time, but she brought it up right after telling us about the divorce."

"I guess that's true. Still doesn't explain who she's supposed to be to me."

"We'll find that out tomorrow," I thought. Sano took back the paper and went to his bed.

Maybe she's actually the reason for the divorce. But if that's the case, Sano shouldn't be the only one involved. If this has something to do with Mom and Dad splitting up, then I deserve to know too.

Chapter 3

Things always came easily to me—math, science, history, every subject I've taken so far. Maybe it's because I'm the son of a multimillionaire who built his success after my granddad suddenly passed away. I can handle both simple and complex problems without much difficulty. I even figured out how to drive when I was ten—though Sano and I got into serious trouble for messing with the car...

But now that I know Mom and Dad aren't how I thought they were, I realize there's still so much I don't understand about people. Dad did his best to shield us, while Mom wanted us to be free. And now that she's leaving, how am I supposed to learn about others if we're trapped in this house?

Ever since we were put on house arrest for sneaking out to the outdoor shopping mall, we've only been allowed to go to school and back. We're finally getting out again—but only because Jay is taking us across town to some restaurant to meet a woman we don't even know.

"I think I came here a few times when I was a teenager. The food's not bad." Jay was talking, but even he had to know the food wasn't exactly our main concern right now.

It was four in the afternoon on a Friday, and we were on our way to do something we still didn't fully understand.

The drive took about twenty minutes, and for once, Jay had nothing to say. No matter how much we wanted answers, we knew the only way to get them was to meet this woman—whoever she was—just like Mom wanted Sano to.

"Okay, boys, it kills me not to tell you everything right now. Like I said before, I'm still getting all the details myself. For now, I'm just following instructions," Jay admitted.

We pulled into the restaurant and stepped inside. It was packed, but that was expected on a Friday afternoon. This place was famous for its seafood—especially its fresh lobster—so it made sense that people would flock here.

As workers rushed back and forth between the kitchen and the dining area, I kept my eyes peeled for Sasha.

"How many in your party today?" I heard the hostess ask Jay. I glanced at her name badge—Crystal. Not the person we were looking for.

"Three. And, if I may ask, is Sasha around?" Jay leaned in, lowering his voice.

Crystal nodded. "She's on her lunch break right now, but she should be back in a few minutes. May I ask who's looking for her?"

"Just a friend." Jay flashed his signature charm. "And, Crystal, you'd be an absolute gem if you could have her wait on us when she gets back. I'd really appreciate it." He locked eyes with her, the way he always did when he wanted someone to go along with him.

Crystal smiled, blushing. "I'll send her your way. In the meantime, if you'd follow me." She led us to a table and handed out menus. "Your server will be with you shortly." Then, with a wink at Jay, she turned and walked away.

Jay winked back before turning to us. "Jay Charm 101: Lesson Three—be nice and don't be afraid."

Sano, unimpressed, ignored him. "So, you're still not going to tell me who this lady is? Or at least why we're even here?"

Jay sighed and focused on his menu, his expression troubled. "Out of respect for your mother—my wonderful aunt—she doesn't want me saying anything beyond what she's asked me to do. She wants to be the

28

one to explain everything now that we've reached this point. You'll understand soon enough."

An awkward silence settled over our table, blending with the chatter and clinking of silverware around us.

It wasn't until Jay lifted his head, his gaze shifting past me, that the tension broke.

"How are you all doing today?" A warm, friendly voice greeted us. "My name is Sasha, and I'll be your waitress this evening. Can I start you off with some drinks?"

Sano and I turned toward the woman standing before us. Her voice was softer in person, but still welcoming. She had light brown hair pulled neatly into a bun. Her black shirt was tucked into her apron, completing the model employee look. Her smile was warm, and she carried herself with a pleasant confidence.

"Just water for all of us," Jay answered smoothly.

"Alright, I'll be right back with three waters." She disappeared in the same direction she had come from. Sano and I exchanged looks, then turned to Jay.

"That lady…" I started. "Have we met her before?"

Jay shrugged. "It's possible. You meet a lot of people in this world." He knew that wasn't the answer we wanted.

"Now is not the time for sarcasm, Jay. She seems… familiar." I kept searching my memory, trying to place where I might have seen her before. We'd attended countless company events with Mom and Dad. But no matter how hard I tried, I couldn't fit her into any of those memories. Still, something about her felt familiar…

"She gives off such a soft and lovely presence," Jay mused. "Kind of like our dear little Sano, don't you think?"

"Actually… yeah, she kind of does," I admitted.

"I don't know about all of that, but…" Sano trailed off, deep in thought. A few seconds later, his eyes widened. "Wait! I think I

29

remember!" He sat up straighter. "That lady—I think I saw her before, at the—"

"Sorry about the wait," a familiar voice interrupted. Sasha had returned, carrying a tray of water. "Here's your water, sir. And here's... yours..."

She froze mid-motion, her gaze locking onto Sano. The glass hovered inches from the table as her hand trembled slightly. Her eyes widened as if she had seen a ghost, blinking rapidly as she struggled to compose herself.

"I—I'm sorry about that," she stammered. "You just... look like someone I know." Her voice had taken on a nervous edge, though she forced a polite smile. She set my water down with a slight tremor, spilling a few drops in the process.

"Forgive my clumsy hand. Let me clean that up for you." She quickly grabbed a napkin, dabbing at the spill before straightening. "I'll give you all some time to look over the menu." Then she walked off, her usual friendly demeanor intact, but something about her posture felt tense. Sano and I exchanged glances.

"That was... weird," I said slowly.

"I think I've seen her at the house before," Sano murmured, still watching where she had disappeared.

"What? When? Why? Is that why she said you looked familiar?" My questions came out in rapid succession.

"I don't know." He frowned. "It was a long time ago. I was maybe five. I remember seeing her talking with Dad... but then Mom called for me. When I turned back, she was gone."

I turned to Jay. "Did you ever see her around?"

Jay leaned back slightly, tapping his fingers against the table. "Back then, I was still in school, so I wasn't around as much. I can't say I've ever seen her at the house. I'll even go as far as to say I've never met her."

30

"So… she's at least someone Dad knows?" I was trying to piece everything together.

Jay didn't answer. He just stared at his menu. If I wasn't imagining things, he was gripping it a little tighter than usual. Before I could press him further, Sasha returned, her notepad in hand.

"Are you all ready to order?" she asked, her expression composed—but her eyes carefully avoided ours.

"I'll have the lobster special," Jay answered smoothly. Then he glanced at us. "Did you boys see something you wanted?"

"The fish and chips is fine for me," I told her, realizing I hadn't even glanced at the menu. Hopefully, it was an option. This was a seafood restaurant, after all.

"Don't think they make it better than I do," Jay teased. Fish and chips was one of his signature dishes at home. "What about you, Sano? Same thing?"

Before Sano could respond, I noticed something strange. Sasha had taken a step back. I looked up just in time to see her already pale complexion drain even further, as if she'd really seen a ghost. Her hazel eyes darkened, glassy with unshed tears.

"Yeah, sure… I'll have the same thing," Sano said slowly, watching her. She gripped her pen so tightly her knuckles turned white, struggling to jot down our orders.

"Alright… your meals will be out shortly," Sasha murmured, her voice barely above a whisper. Her forced smile didn't quite reach her eyes.

Then—just for a second—she hesitated. She stole another quick glance at Sano before abruptly turning away.

I exhaled, glancing between my brother and Jay. "Does she know us or something? Was it not obvious she was trying not to cry?"

This wasn't just strange anymore—it was unsettling. That lady had to know us. And there was no way it was just from seeing Dad once, years ago.

Jay sighed, muttering under his breath. "Pure torture on her own silver platter. I knew I shouldn't have agreed to this..." He took a slow sip of water, his expression unreadable. Before I could press him for answers, a new voice cut in.

"Hello there. Your orders will be out shortly. In the meantime, can I get you a refill on anything?"

We all turned toward the voice. It wasn't Sasha. The woman standing before us had short black hair and a warm, practiced smile.

"We're fine, thank you," Jay answered smoothly, barely looking up.

"If you need anything, just let me know. My name is Diana, and I'll be happy to help." She smiled just like Sasha had—but Sasha was supposed to be our server. Something was off...

Minutes passed. Our food arrived, but Sasha never returned. She wasn't at any of the other tables either. Jay didn't ask about her. Didn't comment on her sudden disappearance. Dinner could not have been more awkward. For once, Jay—the man who loved the sound of his own voice—stayed quiet.

I barely touched my food, my appetite gone. Sano didn't eat much either. Whatever this was about, it involved him, and the weight of it showed in the way he sat in silence, absently pushing food around his plate. The air between us was thick with unanswered questions.

The drive home was unbearable. Jay still hadn't said much, and Sano might as well not have been there at all. He stared blankly out the window, lost in thought.

And me? I was completely out of the loop. Whoever that woman was, she had more to do with Sano than with me. And yet, I couldn't shake the feeling that I should know more—that I needed to know more.

"Welcome back to the Masidone manor," Jay announced as we pulled into the driveway, his voice hollow. He was trying to lighten the mood, but even he didn't sound convinced. He knew more than he was letting on.

We stepped inside, and before we could even wipe our shoes, Sano bolted up the stairs. I hesitated for half a second before following. Our room was on the main floor, so there was only one place he could be going. Our parents' room.

By the time I caught up, he was already standing in the doorway, staring at Mom. She was in her walk-in closet, folding clothes with careful precision—as if keeping her hands busy could keep her mind off whatever was coming.

"That lady," Sano started, breathless. "Who is she?"

Mom didn't look at him. "Did you all go see her?" Her voice was calm, too calm, as she continued folding.

"This Sasha person… She couldn't be… but…" Sano trailed off, shaking his head. He couldn't finish the sentence—or maybe he didn't want to.

Mom sighed, gripping a shirt tighter in her hands. "Yes," she said softly. "She is." Her head dipped slightly, as if just saying the words pained her. My chest tightened.

"Who couldn't she be?" I demanded, frustration bubbling to the surface. "What's going on?"

Sano exhaled sharply. "That day at the house… when I said I thought I'd seen her before—I was right." His voice was distant, like he was piecing together fragments of a memory. "It started coming back to me while we ate. I remembered hearing part of her conversation with Dad. She was asking to see him. To see her son." He swallowed hard, finally looking at me.

"That son… is me."

The air felt like it had been sucked out of the room. My heart pounded. I stared at him, barely able to process what he'd just said.

"I didn't understand what they were talking about back then. I was just a kid. I walked in on them, and heard a few words. Then Mom called me away, and I never thought about it again."

He turned to her, his voice cracking. "Is she really my mother?"

Mom sat on the bed now, her hands limp in her lap. She looked like she was crying—but there were no tears.

"I'm sorry, sweetie," she whispered. "I never meant to keep this from you."

Sano's hands curled into fists. "But you did! Why?"

I had never seen him like this. Never. And I didn't know what shocked me more—the truth itself, or the way it was breaking him apart right in front of me.

Mom's voice trembled as she twisted her hands together in her lap. "It was difficult. It really was."

Sano's fists tightened at his sides. "Then why?" His voice was sharp, almost shaking. "Why did you pretend to be my real mom? Why did you take care of someone who wasn't yours?"

She exhaled slowly, as if the weight of the truth was crushing her. "Your father told me your mother was out of the picture. I wanted to help raise you. I chose to. Then I found out she was still around, but he thought it was best not to confuse you."

Sano let out a bitter laugh. "Out of the picture?" He shook his head. "As soon as she saw me, she looked like she was going to break down. You don't react like that if you're 'out of the picture.'"

His eyes burned with accusation. "Did you keep her away on purpose? Was she not allowed here? What did she do that was so horrible that you all decided I shouldn't even know she existed?"

I had never seen him like this—his voice so raw, his body so rigid with emotion.

34

I didn't dare move. Even the smallest shift felt like it would shatter whatever fragile control he had left. Mom finally broke. A single tear slid down her cheek.

"I just… don't know what to say," she whispered. "It was really hard. All these years…"

Sano inhaled sharply, his hands trembling. "Was it really that hard?" His voice cracked, pain cutting through every syllable. "For you both to pretend like we were some perfect, happy family while you lied to me? You know, I always felt like there was something different between me and everyone else." His chest rose and fell with shaky breaths.

"Turns out I shouldn't have been here."

A heavy silence fell between them.

"Sano…" I turned to see Jay standing behind us. I hadn't even heard him come in.

Sano's lips pressed into a thin line. "I was kept from my real mother. And now, after all this time, I find out she's been suffering while you've been trying to teach me what a 'real family' is supposed to be." He let out a hollow laugh. "Dad is never here. And now you're leaving."

His voice dropped lower, rough with emotion. "If you were really sorry… things wouldn't be like this."

Jay stepped forward, forcing a smile that didn't reach his eyes. "Come on, Sano. Let's go to the kitchen. Kenny-kens and I could use some dessert." He reached for Sano's shoulder, but didn't move. His gaze stayed locked on Mom, searching for something—anything. But she only glanced at him briefly before looking away.

His jaw tightened. His hands curled into fists at his sides. Then, finally, he turned and walked out the door. Jay let out a slow breath before following.

I hesitated, looking between them and Mom. Her head was bowed, her shoulders tense, as if bracing for something she knew wouldn't come. Then I turned and trailed behind them.

Maybe Sano had said too much. Or maybe... he'd just said everything we had all been thinking.

Had he known all along that something wasn't right? Had he been carrying these feelings for years but never spoken up?

We reached the kitchen, and Jay sighed, his voice quieter now. "My heart is broken. It pains me to see you all like this. But you have to know... she's hurting more than you realize."

Sano didn't respond. He stopped at the island counter and leaned forward, resting his arms against the cool surface. His head hung low. His gaze fixed on nothing.

"There's no such thing as a happy family without facing trials together," Jay said, his voice softer than usual. "Real family is about helping each other through the hard times, accepting the flaws we all have. I'm not asking you to understand today, tomorrow, or even next week. But please... don't hate her for this."

Sano didn't react. His gaze remained fixed on the table.

Jay exhaled. "I'm not saying this as her nephew. I'm saying it because I know how much she truly loves you."

For a long moment, Sano was silent. Then, finally, he spoke. His voice was low. "If you were me, how would you feel?"

Jay set down a few bowls for dessert, pausing before answering.

"To be honest? I'd feel the same," he admitted. "Lied to. Confused. Angry." He sat down, resting his elbows on the counter. "But before jumping to conclusions, we should wait. Talk about it with your mother and Papa Masy when everything settles a little. Everything is sort of happening all at once."

Sano scoffed, shaking his head. "Wait for what? Dad had thirteen years to say something. Why would he now?"

Jay hesitated. "...I'm sure he has his reasons." Even he didn't sound convinced.

Dad never acted strange. Never hinted at a secret like this. Would he say something now that we knew the truth? A thought hit me, and I spoke before I could stop myself.

"So then... we're only half-brothers?"

Jay turned to me. "Technically, yeah. But you two are like peanut butter and jelly. No one would ever think you weren't regular siblings."

"There's nothing regular about us," Sano muttered.

Jay opened his mouth to respond, but before he could, a soft voice interrupted. One of the maids had stepped into the kitchen.

"Mr. Davis," she addressed Jay. "The president would like to see the young Masidone." She turned her attention to Sano.

"I didn't know he was back home," Jay said.

"He arrived about thirty minutes ago and has been in his office," the maid replied. "He heard the commotion and would like to see him."

I glanced at Sano. "Are you going to go?"

No response. He didn't even lift his head. Jay stepped in. "Tell him he'll be there soon."

The maid nodded and left.

Jay exhaled, watching Sano carefully. "He would normally page me on the walkie," he murmured. "Seems like he knows we're all caught up now and wants to talk."

I tried to reassure Sano. "You didn't do anything wrong. It should be okay."

Still no response. Then, without a word, Sano straightened and walked out of the kitchen.

Jay sighed. "I'm going to make sure he gets there." He followed.

I wanted to go, too. But something told me my presence wouldn't help. Not this time.

To think I believed we were always close. All this time, he felt different. He remembers seeing his real mom when he was five. He's known for years that something was off, and yet I never had a clue. Mom always did everything for both of us.

The look on her face just now—it was one I've never seen before. What is she thinking? Since Sano and Jay went to see Dad, I decided to check on her.

Everything is falling apart, but I still can't stand to see her like this. I went up to her room, but before I could knock, I noticed the door was open a crack. She was on the phone.

"You know he's smarter than your average teen. I can't imagine what he must be feeling. I can't tell him Kenneth forced her to give him custody. That would make this so much worse." She went quiet, unaware that I was standing at the door.

Then, her voice dropped lower. "I knew he was seeing someone else," she admitted. "But I only found out last week that he was still with this woman. I just can't take it anymore. I've felt so trapped and suffocated. It's time for me to move on—since he already has."

My stomach twisted. Backing away quietly, I headed to my room. I didn't want to hear any more. I glanced at the clock on my desk. Just after seven.

A little over twenty-four hours ago, our biggest worry was getting through our punishment. Now, my parents are splitting up, Sano isn't my full brother, and a woman on the other side of the city is his real mother.

And why is this all happening so suddenly? The father I admired—strict but accomplished—has been deceiving us all along. How am I supposed to face him now? The Masidone family, the one I was so proud to be a part of, isn't even a real family anymore.

I lay in bed, lost in thought. Time blurred. An hour must have passed before I heard the door open. Sano was back.

"That was a long talk," I said as he walked past me and sat on his bed. He didn't answer right away.

Then, finally— "I finished talking to him a while ago. I was on the back porch for a bit."

"What did he say?"

Sano exhaled, rubbing his temples. "He said he was sorry. Then he asked if I wanted to meet her again—this time when she's not working."

"Are you going to?"

"I don't know. I want to, but…" His voice trailed off.

"But what?"

He hesitated, staring at the floor. "That memory… it's the only time I can remember seeing her. I don't know if she ever came by again after that. What if I'm wrong? What if she never meant to see me again?"

"You don't know that for sure. There has to be a reason. Maybe you should ask her?" I suggested.

I kept thinking about the look on Sasha's face. The way she froze when she heard his name. She wouldn't have reacted like that if she didn't want to see him.

"I don't even know what to say about all this. It's so unexpected." I ran a hand through my hair. "Are you going to hate Mom and Dad for this?"

"I don't know," he muttered.

"You don't know?"

"Yeah. I don't know." His voice was sharp now. "Just the other day, everything was fine—our parents, our lives, the way things were. Now, Mom is leaving us, I apparently have another mother, and Dad doesn't even seem bothered by this mess at all. So yeah, I don't know what to feel. Are you fine with all of this?"

"No, I'm not! I'm just as confused as you are."

Sano let out a bitter laugh. "Why? You know who your mom is." His words hit me harder than I expected. It took me moment to respond.

"That doesn't mean I think this is all okay. Finding out our parents are splitting up, that we've been lied to all this time, and that my only brother isn't really my full brother—it's a lot to process."

"And after knowing all that… do you still love them the same?"

I stayed quiet. I was still figuring that out myself.

Sano's eyes darkened. "So, you don't understand." He pushed off the bed and stood. "If you can't tell me that something has changed for you, then you don't get what I'm feeling." His words stung, but I couldn't argue.

Sano crossed the room, yanking open his dresser drawer. He grabbed something—I couldn't tell what—and shut it.

"I'm going out back." He didn't wait for a response. The door closed behind him. I let out a slow breath.

It wasn't that I felt the same as before. It was just… putting into words how betrayed I suddenly felt by my parents was hard.

Chapter 4

That was possibly the longest night I've ever had.

It's Saturday morning now. Usually, Sano, Jay, and I make breakfast together. But today, Jay left early with Mom, and Sano is still in bed. I heard him shifting around a lot last night, so he probably didn't sleep much. I didn't, either. Sleeping in wasn't happening for me, so I was up alone this morning.

"Good morning, young Masidone. Mr. Davis is out at the moment. Would you like us to prepare your breakfast?" I walked into the kitchen and saw two of the maids cleaning.

"Sure," I answered. I didn't really have much of an appetite, but they started making breakfast anyway.

Not only is Dad strict with us and his company, but also with the house. He hired enough staff to ensure someone was always available at any time. They stick to exactly what they're told to do and leave when they're done. Sometimes, they try to make small talk, but I wasn't in the mood for it right now.

"I'll be in the dining room," I told them. They could bring the food there when it was ready. Hopefully, by then, I'd actually want it.

Just as I walked out of the kitchen, Dad walked in.

"Dad, you're home?"

"Does that surprise you?" he chuckled. It did. I hadn't seen him since yesterday morning—before finding out everything.

"Ladies, if you don't mind, I'll take over from here."

The maids exchanged confused glances but stepped aside.

"Excuse us, then." They left, whispering to each other. They weren't wrong to be confused—Dad rarely stops food from being made, whether he's around or not.

"Why did you send them away?" I asked.

"I thought about how long it's been since we made our famous Masidone flapjacks and figured, why not make some for a change?"

"You stopped working to make pancakes?"

"Are you unhappy with my decision? I would've thought you'd enjoy making the pancakes you love so much."

"It's not that I wouldn't want them…" I trailed off. Food wasn't what I wanted right now. I wanted answers. But he was acting as if nothing was wrong.

"So, what kind do you want to make? I believe we still have some blueberries left," he said, looking through the refrigerator.

"Actually, Dad, I want to ask you something."

"While you ask your question, grab the mixing bowl for me." He pointed to the cabinet.

He was as calm as always. No matter the situation, he never lost his composure. I guess that's what made him so intimidating to others— it was almost impossible to tell what he was thinking.

"Well," I started after handing him the bowl, "it's about what we found out yesterday. Why did you never tell us about Sano?"

I braced myself for his response. I needed to hear the reason he had kept this from us. He kept searching through the cabinets, grabbing ingredients as if I hadn't said anything.

"Dad?" I called again.

"Son, what do you call the things I have in front of me?" he asked suddenly. He stood at the island counter, arranging the ingredients he had taken out.

"Pancake mix?"

"Yes, pancake mix. That would be correct… if this were pancake mix," he said. I frowned and looked at the counter again.

"What do you mean?"

"What I mean is, I've gathered these ingredients and have a plan for them. In the end, they will become the mix we need for pancakes. But right now, they're just separate ingredients—simply spices of sorts," he said, gesturing to everything.

I knew he was getting at something, but I wasn't sure what.

"Why do you have pepper out? We never use that." I pointed at the container sitting among the other ingredients.

"Yes, the pepper. I must have grabbed it by mistake. It's good you noticed I didn't need it. If I had used it, the outcome would have been different, right?" He picked up the pepper and put it back in the cabinet.

"Now that that's taken care of, we can successfully make our pancakes using the original recipe we planned to follow."

"Dad, we've made these before. Why are you saying all this?" I asked.

"It's been a while since we last made them, right? Just wanted to remind you of the recipe. I also want you to remember that changing a recipe can sometimes improve the final product. But other times, straying from the original plan leads to undesirable results. That's why it's best to stick with the intended path and leave deviations where they belong." He started mixing the ingredients.

"Okay, but none of that answers my question," I told him. We've followed this same recipe forever. Why was he suddenly talking about the importance of sticking to routine?

He stopped stirring and placed his hands on the table.

"Listen, Ken, you're still young and have your whole life ahead of you. There are infinite things to learn and do—and just as many ways for things to go wrong. I will apologize to you, just as I've already apologized to Sano. This is something you both should have known. But it was decided that it wouldn't be shared."

"And why was that decided? Why couldn't you tell us?"

"Knowing or not knowing wouldn't have changed what's happening now. And what's happening now is that Sano will be meeting Sasha next week to talk."

"Don't you think it's only fair for us to know why you kept something as important as his mother a secret? Sano is really upset by this—I am too," I said, trying to get him to understand.

"I think what's more important for you right now is to focus on your own mother," he said.

"What about my mother?"

"You already know. She'll be moving out soon. I intended to give you more notice, but she told me the other day that she'll be leaving on Monday."

My heart sank. I knew she was leaving soon, but I hadn't realized it would be that soon. Hearing him say it made it all the more real. In just two days, my mom would be gone.

"I know. She said she'd be going soon. She also said we can see her whenever we want."

"And you can. I have no intention of stopping you from visiting her."

"What if I wanted to live with her?" The question slipped out before I could stop it. We had already agreed to stay here, but I wanted to know what he thought about it.

"I suppose when everything was decided, we assumed you both would be fine here. Would you really rather move out with her?"

"Would you be okay if I did?"

Silence filled the air. He stopped what he was doing and turned to face me at the counter. My father rarely took time to respond—he always knew exactly what to say. I braced myself for his answer.

"Ken, you are my son, and I will always love you, no matter what you decide. No matter how much I want you to stay, I will give you the choice, right here and now—to either stay here with me or live with your mother. What do you want to do?" His voice was steady, but the stern look in his eyes told me he expected an answer.

He wants me to choose which parent to stay with. That's pretty much like asking me who I love more. How am I supposed to answer that without hurting anyone? I don't even know if there's a right answer. The only thing I do know is—I don't want my parents to split at all.

It's Saturday morning. We should be making breakfast and joking around like always. But instead, Sano is still sleeping, trying to shut out everything we learned yesterday. He doesn't know I'm here with Dad, being asked to make an impossible choice. And after finding out Mom isn't actually his mother, Sano probably wouldn't want to stay with her anyway.

He snapped at me last night, asking if I was okay with all of this. Of course, I'm not okay. Nothing about this is okay. But what can we do? Just like Dad said, we can't change what's already happened. He probably wouldn't be as successful in business if he let himself break down over everything that went wrong.

Mom's been acting strange for a while now, but as I watch Dad calmly make pancakes, I can't help but wonder—who's really in the wrong here?

"Are you thinking about what you're going to do?" Dad asks, breaking my thoughts.

"Do you love Mom?"

He pauses, caught off guard. "What's brought that on all of a sudden?"

"I just want to know." I hesitate, searching for the right words. "Nothing seemed this bad last week. And now... all of this. She's not

45

herself anymore. So I just... I just want to know." I might be crossing a line, but his face shows he's actually considering his answer.

"I loved your mother dearly," he finally says. "But as we've come to this point, that wasn't enough. And to keep our lives steady, we decided it was best to go our separate ways."

I swallow hard. "What about Sano's mom? Did you love her too?"

His brow lifts slightly, like he didn't expect that question.

"I should have known you'd ask me that," he says, his expression easing as he goes back to cooking.

"If you hid her from us, that must mean you didn't, right? Or were you still seeing her without telling anyone?" I think back to what I heard Mom say on the phone—that he was still with someone else. Could she have meant Sano's mom?

Dad doesn't stop cooking, but his tone is steady when he finally answers. "Sasha and I haven't spoken in quite some time."

"Is that why she looked so surprised to see us?" I ask. "She looked at Sano like she'd just seen a ghost. She was so shocked she didn't even finish serving us. I've never seen someone change like that so fast."

Dad's expression tightens. "If it were up to me, you wouldn't have gone to that restaurant." His words come out sharper than before. "If I had known, I would have stopped you immediately. It was your mother's decision to let you meet her so hastily."

"She seemed like a nice lady. I don't get why you never told us about her."

"Ken." His voice is short and firm. Whenever he says my name like that, it means I've said too much. That he wants this conversation to end. I wanted to be done too. But every time I thought about Mom leaving and the way Sano's mom looked at him, I couldn't let it go.

"Did she do something so terrible that you had to go through all this trouble? Having Mom pretend to be his mother too?" I press. "As soon as she told us about the divorce, she told us about her. Why was it so easy for Mom to tell us, but you never planned to?"

His jaw tightens. "Your mother had no business telling you any of this. I have no idea why she so rashly thought to tell you." His voice drops slightly, more measured. "Now that it's come to this, I can't keep her away anymore."

"But that's just it—why did you keep her away in the first place? You still haven't answered that."

Dad's hands still. Then, in a clipped tone, he says, "Ken." His voice has an edge now. "There is a time and a place for everything. Right now is neither the time nor the place for this conversation."

I opened my mouth, but he cut me off before I could say anything.

"When—and if—the time comes, you'll know what you need to know. You're still young, and not everything makes sense yet. Once you're older and have done a bit more maturing, you'll start to understand why people handle things differently than you expect."

Other than the batter sizzling in the skillet, the kitchen was silent. I knew I was still young. I knew I might not understand everything he did. But something like this? There couldn't be a good enough reason to hide the truth. And yet... my dad has never steered me wrong before. Maybe there is a reason.

I don't spend enough time around people to really understand them—at least, not outside of our family. Just like that girl we met at the mall. I didn't know anything about her, and I ended up saying something that really upset her. If I had known better, I wouldn't have said what I did.

Dad barely glanced at me. "The look on your face tells me you understand." His voice was steady, unreadable. "You have two options from here on out. You can keep dwelling on something that's out of your control, or you can enjoy some Masidone flapjacks and move forward as we work through this adjustment period."

As he spoke, he placed a plate of fresh pancakes in front of me. The conversation was over. There was nothing else I could say to make him understand me. Nothing else I could do to change the way things were. So that left me with option two.

Accept it. Move on.

At least for now.

Chapter 5

Trying to enjoy breakfast with Dad was impossible. I had no appetite, and forcing myself to sit at the dining table, pretending otherwise, felt like torture. He ate in silence, eyes fixed on his laptop, while I sat there, holding the same piece of pancake on my fork, unmoving. There wasn't much else to say.

I didn't feel like making small talk, so the only thing left between us was awkward silence.

"I'm thinking about adding some upgrades to the house," he said, taking a sip of his coffee. "Let me know if there's anything you'd like. I remember you once saying you wanted a bathroom in your game room. That way, when you and Sano pull all-nighters, you wouldn't have to go down the hall. I can have that built in. I'm also planning to add another hallway from the living room to my office—should make getting around easier."

"Yeah, sure," I muttered, barely paying attention.

I didn't care about adding a bathroom, a hallway, or whatever else he wanted to change in the mansion. He barely used half the place anyway—just his office, his room, and here. So what was the point?

"If there's anything else you want, let me know," he added, gathering his plate. "I'll be in my office until your mother gets back with Jayson." He left, then returned a minute later to grab his laptop before heading down the hall.

I waited long enough to be sure he was closed off in his office before taking my plate to the kitchen. Then, I headed back to my room. Sano was finally awake, sitting up in bed.

"You just got up?" I asked.

"No, I've been up since you left."

"You have? Dad and I made breakfast. You should've come to get some if you were awake."

"I knew that's where you were," he said flatly. "It's Saturday. But since Jay didn't come in to wake us up, I figured he wasn't here. I didn't feel like talking to Dad, so I just stayed."

"Why are you holding your phone like that?"

I couldn't help but notice the way Sano's fingers clenched tightly around his cell. He didn't even seem to realize it until I pointed it out. His eyes flickered to his hand, and he loosened his grip slightly.

"You alright?" I walked over to his side, but he kept his head down, focused on the screen.

"I called her again."

"Her?" I hesitated. "You mean… your mom?"

"Yeah."

"What did she say?"

"She couldn't speak." His voice was quiet. "She just… kept crying. The only thing she managed to say was that she had to go. Same thing happened yesterday."

I blinked. "You called her yesterday too?"

"When I went back outside," he admitted. "I needed to hear it from her directly—that she really is my mother. When she finally said yes, she lost it. And when she got herself together, all she could say was, 'Goodnight, Sano. I have to go.'" His grip tightened around his phone again.

I had no idea he'd been calling her. We had only just met her yesterday, and he was already reaching out. I didn't think he'd want to contact her so soon.

Sano exhaled sharply. "No matter where we went, what we did, or how we acted, something always felt... off. I never knew why. But now... I get it."

There was something in his voice—a kind of realization that shouldn't have been realized.

"Why didn't you tell me you felt that way?" I asked, sitting on the edge of my bed.

"I don't know." He finally set his phone down, rubbing his hands together as if trying to shake off the tension. "I thought I was crazy for thinking it. No one ever acted weird or said anything that made me think something was wrong, so I didn't want to say anything in case I was just imagining it." He looked over to me.

"You never thought it was weird? That even though we do everything together, we're still so different? That I barely resemble Dad and look nothing like Mom? That my name is nothing like yours? And what about our birthdays?" He shook his head. "That was the biggest one. I'm only seven months older than you. Unless we were taught wrong, that shouldn't be possible. Has that never crossed your mind?"

I felt myself sinking deeper into my bed. The weight of his words settled in. I never had a reason to question anything before. I thought our lives were normal. We played, went to school, got in trouble—just like any other kids. Sure, Dad was overprotective, but that just seemed like a parent thing.

But now... was it really just that? Could he have been shielding Sano? Or even me? Mom was never as strict—was there another reason for that too? Now, I had just as many questions as Sano. And from Dad's refusal to talk, I had a feeling I wouldn't be getting any answers anytime soon.

"I can't believe I never realized," I finally said.

"It's not really something for you to realize," Sano replied. "This is your family. All of it—Dad, Mom, Jayson... everyone. Of course, everything felt normal to you—you came from all of them. I didn't. I came from a teacher and a part-time waitress."

We were always told we were too smart for our age. So, of course, Sano would notice things like this. But why didn't I? I couldn't shake the thought that I had been blind to something I should have known. Sano was only seven months older than me. We lived in the same room, under the same roof. How could there be such a big difference between us?

"Knock, knock."

Sano was already looking up when I turned to see Jay standing in the doorway.

"Sorry I missed breakfast. I just got back with Kelly," he said, stepping into the room.

"Where did you guys go so early?" I asked. It was only ten o'clock. Mom rarely went anywhere before noon.

"She wanted to show me her new place." Jay hesitated, like he didn't really want to answer.

"Where is it?" I asked, even though I wasn't sure I wanted to know. Right now, the only thing I wanted was answers to everything I didn't know.

"She's moving into the same apartment building as my dear mother." He sighed. "I think she should live close to someone right now. I don't know if she told you, but by the time you two get home from school Monday, most of her stuff will be gone. And so will she."

"Yes, I get it. She's leaving." I'd already heard it once today. I'd been hearing it since she first mentioned it the other day. It wasn't something I wanted to be constantly reminded of.

"Kenny-Kens…" Jay looked like he wanted to say something else, but for once, he didn't. The world must've stopped spinning—because if Jay was at a loss for words, that meant the situation was bad.

"Can I ask you something, Jay?" Sano's voice pulled both of us back to reality.

"You can ask me anything," Jay said without hesitation.

"Why did you decide to move out? You were only eighteen, right? Then you came back... but now you're staying with us instead of your own parents."

Jay ran a hand through his hair, exhaling.

"I had no issues with my parents. I just... had something I wanted to go for." He glanced away. "When I was with... you know."

We both knew who he meant.

"We were doing well with our acting. I was supposed to go with her to L.A. when she got that film offer. My mom was against it, but I wanted to be with her. So, I moved in with her while we finished college." His voice dipped lower. "But then she left without me. And I had nowhere else to go. I couldn't bear crawling back to my mother in the state I was in."

His shoulders tensed before he forced a small smile.

"Kelly came and got me. Said staying with you guys was more than okay."

Jay had been living with us for almost two years now. I'd known him my whole life, but it wasn't until he moved in that I truly got to know him. He was a complete wreck. I never imagined someone— especially Jay—could be so depressed and disconnected from the world. I don't know the full story of why his ex-girlfriend did what she did, but whatever it was, it really messed him up for a while.

"If you wanted to, could you move back with them even though you went against them?" I wasn't sure why Sano was asking these questions, but the serious look on his face told me he really wanted an answer.

"Again, I had no issues with my mother. Even though she didn't agree with me moving to L.A. to pursue acting, she still supported me.

She would have taken me back at any time. But knowing she hadn't wanted me to go in the first place, I couldn't face her—not after proving her right. She always sensed something was off about Amy, but I was too blind to see it. And by the time I did, it was too late." Jay fell silent.

"Sorry, I didn't mean to bring her up." Even though we didn't know the full story about Amy, she was still a taboo subject in the house—it had affected Jay too much.

"No, no, it's okay. You wanted to know something. She just happened to be part of that answer." Jay took a deep breath. "But what made you ask?"

"I don't know. I just got curious," Sano muttered, looking back down at his phone.

"I know it's hard to understand. Your parents' divorce is one thing, but this situation with your biological mother… it's going to take time to process. I'm sure Papa Masy already told you that you'll be meeting her this coming week. So, let's just see what happens, yeah?" Jay asked hopefully.

Sano didn't respond. He was never that talkative, but now he seemed even more distant than usual.

"Mind if I come in?"

We all turned to see my mom standing by the door. I hadn't seen her since yesterday. Her usually cheerful eyes were puffy. The long hair she let flow and bounce when she walked was pulled back into a ponytail. She wasn't wearing her favorite cashmere sweater—the one she always wore on cool Saturday mornings. For a second, I wasn't sure if I was even looking at my mother.

"How are you boys today?" She stepped in slowly.

"They're… in recovery," Jay answered for us. I was relieved. I didn't want to keep her waiting for an answer neither of us wanted to give.

"I figured as much." She sighed. "We just got back from seeing the place where I'll be staying. I was wondering if you wanted to help me move."

Jay looked at her. I did too. Did she really want us to help her leave?

"I'll be packing the rest of today, so I thought maybe you could help me move my things when I'm all set. But if you don't want to, I understand." She looked uneasy.

I didn't exactly want to help her leave. But I didn't want to miss the chance to see her before she went.

"You're leaving Monday, right? We have school," I reminded her.

"You never miss school as it is. One absence won't hurt." She tried to joke, offering a small smile. I wondered how many more of those I'd get to see.

"Kelly, could you give us a little more time? I'll let you know what they decide," Jay told her.

"Alright, Jayson. I'll talk to you boys later. If you need anything, just let me know." She slowly turned and walked out. I couldn't help but wonder if that would be the last time I saw my mom walk out of my room.

"Why did you send her away?" I asked.

"I know my aunt. And because I know her, I couldn't bear to see her break down in front of you two. She's a strong woman, but even she has a limit. This whole thing is really hard on her. You're her kids. She wants to be in your life, but now that they're separating, it'll be harder for her to be around all the time."

"So," Sano spoke slowly, "it'll be just like with my mom, then?"

"That... is a separate matter. What happened with them is different," Jay said.

"What did happen? Why can't I know why Dad made it so I never saw her?"

"I wish I could answer that, but honestly, I think you'd be better off not knowing."

"Better off?" Sano scoffed. "You sound just like him. You're taking his side on this?"

"It's not like that, Sano."

"Don't say my name," he demanded. "It's a constant reminder that I'm not supposed to be here. I'm sorry. I can't just accept this so easily, no matter how much you want me to. I might have only seen her yesterday, but knowing she's wanted to see me this whole time—knowing she cries every time I try talking to her—it's hard to accept that she's been kept away from me all these years, and no one said a thing."

"I know. I'm not asking you to accept it. But Kelly is moving out in a couple of days. I don't want to make this any harder on her than it already is."

"She was the one who told me. She brought it up. She should have known I wouldn't be okay finding out she's been lying to me my whole life. Especially after that time." Sano's fists clenched at his sides. "I feel like she knew my mother was here, and that's why she called me away—in case I saw her. She didn't want me to know. They both did so much to keep me in the dark." He turned his back to us.

Jay and I exchanged a look. There was nothing else to say. It was no secret this was going to be hard for Sano. For all of us. Except Dad. He's the only one acting like everything is fine.

Why doesn't he see how much this is upsetting everyone? The only thing he seems to care about is the fact that Mom told us about his mother—not how we feel about it. I don't even care about what happened in the past. Because looking at things now, trying to move on like everyone wants us to won't be easy.

Chapter 6

It had been a really long weekend. I was the only one who went with Mom to help her move. Sano decided to go to school. I didn't want to leave him, but I couldn't leave Mom either. I hated feeling like I had to choose between helping my brother and helping my mom, but after today, I'd still be living with Sano...

"Can you put that box in the living room?" Mom asked.

I set the box down next to the couch. The living room and dining area shared the same space, with the kitchen visible from both. Her two bedrooms were almost the size of mine combined. This whole apartment could probably fit inside our dining room.

"Kells, why did you buy so much stuff? You know it's just you, right?" My aunt Jamie walked in carrying a large floor lamp. She lived in the apartment upstairs, so she came to help with the move.

"You know how I get when I see things I like. It's only a little more, I promise." Mom held her fingers close together, showing a tiny gap—despite the fact that half the moving truck was still full.

"I guess we'll be alright since we got little man here to help us," Aunt Jamie said, glancing at me. "But where's Sano? He isn't helping too?"

"He couldn't miss school," Mom lied. We both knew Sano had chosen to go to school instead of coming here.

"Well, we've got one little rebel with us, so we should be fine." Aunt Jamie winked at me. She and my mother were close. She knew what was going on, and I was sure she saw right through Mom's lie. But she didn't push. Instead, she kept unpacking, putting things where they belonged.

"He's really growing up. He's taller than you now," Aunt Jamie noted.

"Well, he's certainly not getting his height from a five-six woman like me," Mom chuckled.

"I know. It's that giant father of his. What is he—six-two, six-three?"

"Something like that."

Mom and Aunt Jamie talked about my father like nothing was wrong. Like she wasn't moving in here because they were having problems. Like they weren't separating.

"Ken definitely has a lot more growing to do. Don't forget about us little people when you shoot up," Mom teased.

She was trying to joke, trying to act like everything was fine. But part of me was struggling to pretend along with her.

"Even if I grew to be twice your height, I'd never forget about you," I told her.

I wasn't sure if she was putting on an act or if she really believed things would be okay. Either way, I couldn't just go along with it. After today, I didn't know when I'd be able to visit again.

Mom paused, setting down the box she was holding. Aunt Jamie, standing behind her, also stopped.

"Kells, I'm going to start bringing in your bedroom stuff," she said before stepping outside.

Mom walked over to me, placing her hands gently on my face. "Ken," she said, her voice soft, "you know that I love you, right?"

"I do."

"Good. Don't you dare forget that. I may be moving here, but that doesn't change a thing—not with you, not with Sano. I love you both no matter what. I've said it before, and I'll say it again: you're both welcome here, any day, any time. Don't ever forget that, okay?"

"I won't, Mom."

"Good." She pulled me into a hug. I hugged her back, holding on just a little longer. Mom had always been there for me, always had my back. It was going to be different now. I had to stay strong for her so she wouldn't keep worrying about me.

"I wish Sano had come with you," she admitted. "But I understand—he's confused right now. I won't force him to do anything, but please remind him of what I said. I've always considered him my son, and I always will."

Even after everything, she was still thinking about Sano.

"I'll let him know," I assured her.

She looked at me and smiled. A real smile—the first one I'd seen since all of this started. I was glad I got to see it before leaving.

The day had dragged on, and by the time I got back home, it was late. Jay had come to pick me up from Mom's place. She still had things to unpack, but everything was in. Before we left, Jay got a chance to talk with his mom, and Mom and I said our goodbyes—until next time.

Time didn't seem to be in a hurry these days. The night stretched on endlessly, and the next day felt like it wasn't moving at all.

No one had told me Sano was going to meet his mother again today. He went right after school—without me. Now, I was just waiting to hear how it went.

He said she always cried when he spoke to her. I wondered how she was doing now. What were they talking about? Would he keep going to see her, the way I'd keep visiting Mom?

Sitting in my room like this, flipping through my schoolbooks, was hard. Jay was with him. Mom was gone. Dad was in his office. I had no one to go to right now.

My school friends kept their distance—they knew my background. Others got too close, too nosy. But hanging out with anyone didn't feel right anyway. I just wanted things at home to go back to how they were.

But maybe that was impossible.

I turned a page in my social studies book when my phone vibrated. A text from Jay.

—*Headed back your way. Will be there soon.*

—*Give Sano some space. I'll fill you in later.*

The messages felt... off. Jay usually put more into his texts. These were rushed, clipped, like he was trying to be quick and discreet. Something must have happened for him to give me this heads-up.

They'd only been gone a couple of hours. I thought they'd be out longer.

I lost the little bit of focus I had left and shut my book. My eyes drifted to Sano's side of the room. The only real friend I had, apart from Jay. Seeing him like this had me worried, but what could I do?

About twenty minutes passed. Then I heard a noise from my desk drawer.

I opened it and saw my walkie-talkie—the one I used to reach Jay when I didn't feel like tracking him down. It beeped three times in a row, then once, then three more times.

Our code for help. They must be back. I rushed out of my room, heading straight for the entrance. Just as I got there, the door swung open.

"We're back," Jay said. His tone was even, flat. No usual cheer in his voice. Not a good sign.

"How'd everything go?" I asked, scanning behind him. No sign of Sano.

Jay gave a slow shake of his head. Before I could react, Sano slipped past both of us, like I wasn't even there.

I turned to follow him, but Jay's hand landed on my shoulder, stopping me.

"Please, he needs a little space right now," Jay told me, throwing his head to the left—down the hall toward his room. I took that as a sign to follow, so I did.

Once we reached his room, he shut the door and let out a long exhale.

"I thought the meeting at the restaurant was terrible, but this... this was just awful." He turned to me, shaking his head.

"What happened?"

"We met at this juice bar not far from the school she teaches at. Everything was going well. But then... she showed up." He paused, heading to his walk-in closet to hang up his jacket.

"As soon as she saw him again, I could already see the tears forming in her eyes. She took a deep breath before walking over to us. I tried to get the conversation going, but Sano just... sat there. Watching her. Not saying a word." Jay walked over to his desk, where I was sitting.

"Then, finally, Sano spoke—cutting off our conversation with just one word. 'Mom.'"

He let the word hang in the air for a moment before continuing.

"She just looked at him. Like she couldn't believe it. Maybe it was the first time he'd ever called her that. I saw it coming and handed her some napkins. She wiped her face and tried to speak, but that... that was harder to watch than her crying."

"Did she not like that he called her that?" I asked.

Jay hesitated, running a hand through his hair before answering.

"She asked him to say it again. And when he did, she grabbed his hands and just... held them. I figured it wasn't my place to say anything, so I let them have their moment. She finally pulled herself together and started asking him questions—nothing too deep. Just the usual 'How are you?' 'How's school?' stuff like that. It took him a while, but eventually, he answered. Things started flowing from there."

"You guys came back a lot sooner than I expected. Did she have to leave?"

Jay sighed, his eyes distant for a moment.

"Well… once they got past the small talk, Sano must have found the strength to ask the question that had been weighing on him." Jay's expression darkened. "He asked her what happened. Why she wasn't around." He swallowed hard.

"With her condition, I would've stopped him if I'd known he was going to ask that so soon."

"Did she lose it again?"

"It was more than that." Jay's voice dropped to a near whisper, his expression tight. "She just kept apologizing—saying it was all her fault. Then she said she wished she could start over from the beginning and try again."

"Try what again?"

"Trying to keep him in her life." His answer was barely audible. The pain in his eyes said enough. I can't even begin to imagine what Sano must be feeling right now.

"I tried to calm her down, but it was no use," Jay continued. "I told her it might be best to try again another day. She didn't want to leave him again, but she started feeling lightheaded and had no choice but to go home and settle her nerves. That's why we came back so soon. Sano hasn't said a single word since. He's just been staring off into space, his face blank. That's why I told you to give him some space. He needs time to process everything."

"So… I can't talk to him?"

"Any other time, I'd say sure, but there's not much you could say right now that would change anything. It's better to let him think things through until he's ready."

"Why did this have to happen anyway?" Frustration swelled in my chest. "Have you always known about this? How come you never told us?"

"I didn't know. At least, not the whole story." Jay sighed, rubbing the back of his neck. "I knew Kelly only had you, but I thought maybe Sano came from a previous marriage or something. I was younger than you when Papa Masy came around. I wasn't really thinking about stuff like that."

I guess that makes sense, especially since I never questioned anything until now.

"There was one day, about a year ago, after I first came here," Jay continued. "I decided to ask her about him, but she just went quiet. I figured it was better not to push. Then, about a month ago, when she was talking about her doubts with Papa Masy, the subject came up again. That's when she finally started opening up about it."

"And? What did she say?"

"It's... complicated." Jay looked away, his gaze distant.

I clenched my fists, frustration bubbling up. "So, out of everything, this is the one thing you choose not to tell me? Something this important?"

"Kenny-kens, it's not like that," he said, his voice softening. "For one, it's not my story to tell. And besides... it's just not something you're meant to understand right now."

"You sound just like Dad."

"Well, if he said that, he's right. Besides, I never talked to him about this. It's between him and Sano's mother." Jay exhaled heavily. "Even Kelly doesn't—or didn't—know the details of their relationship when everything happened. Just like now..." His words trailed off, and for a moment, my thoughts drifted back to that phone call my mom had.

"Is Dad with someone else?" I asked, though I wasn't really expecting an answer. But Jay let out a troubled sigh and met my gaze.

63

"It's my understanding that he is." His reluctance was evident, but he still said it. A sharp pang hit my chest.

"Honestly, everything right now is a mess," Jay continued. "And I can't just leave you all after everything you've done for me. Kelly may be out, but only out of the house. She'd be here in a flash if you needed her. Papa Masy… may not be much help for a few reasons. One being, he's still in contract negotiations with another business, so he's a little preoccupied."

"He's always a little preoccupied," I muttered, the bitterness seeping into my voice.

Jay nodded. "That's just how he is. Everything has to be done efficiently and precisely."

"And what about us?"

"He's a businessman running a massive company."

"You're saying it's okay for him to ignore us?"

"When did you hear me say that?" Jay asked, brows furrowed in confusion.

"It just feels like you're making excuses for him," I shot back.

"I'm not making excuses," he said, his tone firm but patient. "I just want you to understand that everyone has a story. Your mom has one. So does he. Understanding both helps you find a solution faster—before jumping to conclusions or pointing fingers."

"Oh, so his story is just 'I'm a busy businessman'?" I scoffed. "He gets caught up in work, tears his family apart, keeps Sano's mother away, drives my mom out, and then rides off into the sunset with someone else we don't even know?"

Jay let out a heavy sigh, rubbing his temples in frustration. "That's not exactly what I meant…"

"Then what is it, Jay?" My frustration flared hotter. "I get that you're trying to help, but how can anything get better if I don't even understand what went wrong in the first place?"

"Listen, Kenny-Kens." Jay's voice softened, but it was still steady, serious. "You're smart, perceptive—you've got all of Dad's quick thinking and problem-solving skills. But this… this is something you've never really dealt with before. Relationships. People. Love. And all the mess that comes with it."

I hesitated, a little thrown off by his serious tone.

"You're going to be thirteen soon, but you're still only twelve. And sometimes, even I forget that. You're wise beyond your years, no doubt. But you're also a bit sheltered. You live in this big, beautiful mansion outside the city. You haven't really seen the world yet. So, what I'm trying to say is… this might be one of those things that you won't fully understand right now. But with time, you will. I promise."

Jay only spoke like this when he was being completely serious.

"In no way am I saying what your father did was right," he continued. "In my personal opinion, it was wrong. He should've talked to Kelly first before any of this happened. And as for Sano's mother… that was awful, too. But that's something Papa Masy will have to explain, since it was between them."

"So, in other words, you're telling me I have to grow up before I can say this whole thing is messed up and sucks?"

Jay huffed a quiet laugh. "Well, you can say it now. If it'll make you feel better, I'll say it with you—because this really does suck."

He was trying to joke, trying to lighten things up, but I couldn't bring myself to play along. I knew he was doing his best to keep the balance I wanted back. I just didn't know how he planned to do it. I only hoped he could find a way.

Chapter 7

I didn't bother asking Sano about what happened—Jay had already told me. Instead, I just tried talking to him like normal. He answered when he felt like it, but mostly, he kept to himself. He spent most of his time studying in our room, barely coming out, even for dinner. It was clear he was keeping himself busy just to avoid us.

And that's how it stayed for the rest of the week.

Jay went to visit Mom and Aunt Jamie. I wanted to go with him, but Mom said she wanted everything set up before I came back over. It had been almost a week since she left, and the house wasn't the same anymore. I was the only one who felt that way.

Jay got to see her. Dad hadn't mentioned her once. And Sano… he didn't seem bothered at all.

I walked into our room and found Sano rummaging through his closet.

"What are you doing?" I asked.

"Nothing really. Just looking through all this stuff we have." He flipped through the clothes hanging inside.

I frowned. "Why?"

Sano never really cared about clothes. Like me, he just took whatever we got, without caring about brand names or how much we had.

"They're almost done with dinner. Are you coming to eat?" I asked, since he ignored my first question.

"I want to finish what I'm doing. If I get done, I'll go." He didn't look at me, just kept his head in the closet.

I shifted tactics. "Have you talked to her since then?"

That finally got his attention.

"Yeah, I have." He stopped what he was doing and turned to me.

"Are you going to see her again soon?"

"Yeah. I will."

"That's good." I hesitated, clearing my throat before continuing. "Have you… have you talked to my mom? Since that time?" The last time I knew, he had yelled at her in her room.

"No, I haven't." His voice was flat. "I don't really have anything to say, so there's no reason to talk."

"So… you're still mad at her?"

"I'm not mad. I just don't have anything to say."

"You're not bothered by her moving out? By her not being here anymore?"

"Why should I be?" Sano's voice was steady, but I could hear something beneath it. "It seemed like once her time here was done, her time with me was done too. She didn't waste a second telling me she wasn't my mother anymore."

He turned back to the closet, sifting through his clothes like the conversation didn't matter. But I knew better. He wasn't angry—he was hurt. He thought she had let go of him.

"Well, maybe I should talk to her," he said after a moment. "Thank her for telling me the truth. If she hadn't, who knows if I ever would've found out."

Something about his tone sent a prickle of unease through me. He didn't sound like himself.

"You've got it wrong," I said. "She still cares about you. Talk to her and see for yourself."

Sano let out a sharp breath. "Hard to believe that when she calls you all the time but hasn't called me once. Why should I think she still cares?"

"She asks about you every time. She's just giving you space. She knows you're a little upset and confused, so she wanted to wait until you were feeling better."

"Confused?" He scoffed. "I'm not confused. I get it. She played mommy until she didn't have to anymore. Maybe Dad told her not to say anything, but in the end, she still went behind his back to tell me. And now she doesn't have to come back here to see us. Of course, she'll say she cares—knowing the only way we'd see each other is if I go to visit her."

He turned to me, his expression unreadable. "She may still care about you, but I don't see her feeling the same way about me."

"That's not true," I said firmly. "She wouldn't have done all that for you over the years if she didn't care. Maybe she always wanted to tell you the truth, but Dad stopped her. Maybe this was the only way she could. You know mom. If she didn't like you, it would've been obvious."

Sano huffed, pushing aside another row of clothes. "Feels kind of obvious now," he muttered.

I took a step closer. "So that's it? You're just going to throw her aside after all this time? She cared for you for thirteen years, and that doesn't mean anything?"

"My mom was the one who wanted to care for me for those thirteen years." Sano spun around to face me.

"You didn't see how sad she was when she spoke to me. Or the pain in her voice when she said she wished she could turn back time— back to before I was taken from her. For the first time, I felt like I was really wanted. You know what I've always felt with 'mom'?" He put special emphasis on the word. I stayed silent.

"I always felt... guilt," he continued. "Every time she looked at me, there was this guilt in her eyes—like she just felt bad for me. And I never understood why. I tried my best to be a good kid, to change that look. But here we are. She reached her caring limit and let me go."

He sounded so sure. And the way he said it made it almost believable. But even if there was some truth to it, I knew my mom wouldn't lie about what she told me.

"I didn't expect you to understand," Sano said, his tone hardening. "She's your mom, so of course you're going to take her side. But as my brother—the person who should know me best—I was hoping you'd at least try to see things from my point of view."

He turned away and went back to rummaging through his closet.

I wanted to say something, anything, but nothing felt right. He had it all wrong, but he was so convinced he was right. Maybe this is what Jay meant when he said Sano needed space. Maybe this is why Mom thought he was confused. Right now, there was no getting through to him.

"I'm going to the dining room for dinner," I said finally. "Come when you're ready."

I left before things could get worse. As much as I wanted to fix this, everyone kept saying there wasn't much I could do. I just had to wait and hope things would get better.

Jay glanced up as I walked into the dining room. "I was just about to come looking for you. You usually come running when we tell you food's ready."

I barely had time to respond before I noticed someone else sitting at the table.

"You're eating with us?" I asked, looking at Dad.

"Is that a problem?" he asked, half-smirking.

"No, just... rare." I slid into my seat beside Jay.

"Anna really outdid herself with today's meal," Jay said, nodding toward the table.

Pot roast, potatoes, and mixed vegetables. The rich, savory aroma filled the air, and for the first time all day, I felt a little bit hungry.

"Sano's not joining us?" Dad asked as soon as we sat down.

"He's busy with something," I replied.

"What could be more important than making sure he eats before it gets too late?" he wondered. Even if I knew exactly what Sano was doing, I doubted he'd want me to share.

"You know how us boys can be," Jay said casually.

"Yes, I am aware," Dad said. "But I also know he's not handling things well." He sighed. "He's been skipping a lot of meals lately. He hasn't made himself sick, has he?"

"No, he seems fine to me," I told him.

"At least he's holding up well. You kids are strong. Even when times are tough, you manage to stand on your own." He took a sip of water.

Jay and I exchanged a glance. That just proves how little he's around. If he really paid attention, he'd know how much this was affecting us.

"Good coping skills will serve you well in the future," Dad continued. "This business is no walk in the park. There will be times when your back is against the wall. But as long as you stay levelheaded, you'll do just fine."

"You're talking like I'm already set to take over," I said.

"Of course you are. Who else would be my successor?" He chuckled like I'd just made a joke.

"So… you expect me to take over the company?"

"I was hoping that could be our plan."

The air in the room grew heavy. We hadn't talked about this much before. I always knew he wanted one of us to keep the business going, but just like that, he decided it would be me?

"What about Sano?" I asked. "Would he take over too?"

"He can certainly work there," Dad said. "But there only needs to be one president."

"And you'd rather it be me than him?"

"I wouldn't say 'rather,'" he said. "It's just been decided that you would do it."

"What if he wanted to?"

Dad's expression shifted slightly. "Are you saying you don't?" He studied me, waiting for an answer.

I knew arguing wouldn't change anything, but he should at least explain why me and not Sano. He was older. Shouldn't he be the one in charge?

"I didn't intend to discuss this matter today," Dad said. "You still have plenty of time before I expect you to start learning the ropes." He started eating but paused for a moment, looking up in thought. "Oh my, time is flying. Your birthday's in a couple of weeks, isn't it? Before you know it, you will be the big man in charge."

I usually look forward to my birthday. It's always been a time when we all got together, went somewhere fun, and made good memories. But this year... I'm not so sure I even want to celebrate.

Mom isn't here. Sano isn't himself. And father-son time just doesn't feel the same.

Chapter 8

With each passing day, things were supposed to get easier. They were supposed to gradually get better. But instead, everything felt heavier—more uncertain. Answers seemed further away than ever. And not just answers—people, too.

Night had fallen. Sano and I sat at our desks, working on homework in silence. Normally, he'd ask about something in math, but tonight, his pencil just kept moving across the page. I had been watching him when he finally looked over to me.

"Have you ever done something you regretted?" he asked suddenly.

I frowned. "Why are you asking me that?" His question came out of nowhere, but his tone was serious.

"Just... have you ever thought about doing something crazy, then actually did it, and regretted it?"

I thought for a moment. "Not that I can think of. I wouldn't say I regret anything." There was too much on my mind to give it proper thought.

Then something came to me. "Oh, wait—that time we went to the mall," I said. "After everything that's happened, I've been thinking about how I should act and how I understand people. Since we don't really talk to a lot of regular people—like those girls that time—I should think before I speak. I should be more aware of situations before jumping in. I still kind of feel bad about what I said to that one girl."

I hadn't thought about that incident much, but I hadn't forgotten it either. It was another example proving Jay's point—how I needed to know more about the real world, not just what I thought I knew.

"I thought about that too," Sano admitted. "I'm pretty sure if I'd been the one to say something, I probably would've said something just as dumb."

I shook my head. "I doubt it. You're better at holding your tongue. Apparently, I take after Mom and her 'say whatever's on her mind' habit." I chuckled, but the moment the words left my mouth, I regretted them. I'd been trying my hardest not to bring her up anymore.

"Sorry," I murmured, guilt settling in.

Sano didn't seem bothered, but he had that look—that deep, lost-in-thought expression. His pencil rested loosely in his hand as he stared blankly at nothing in particular.

"What?" I asked, sensing he was in the mood to talk.

"Earlier, when you went to have dinner, I talked to her again."

"You two seem to be talking a lot." I'd never actually seen him on the phone with his mom, but lately, he always seemed to be speaking with her when no one was around.

"Yeah. She's always wanted to talk to me. And after finally getting these chances, I feel like... a part of me that I never understood is becoming clearer," he said, shifting slightly in his chair. "That's why—even though I only found out about her a couple of weeks ago—I still regret not knowing her my whole life."

"That wasn't your fault," I reminded him. "You didn't know. What could you have done about something you had no way of knowing?"

"But I still had that feeling," he murmured. "Something I could've questioned long ago, but never did."

"They probably wouldn't have told you anyway," I said, the words heavy on my tongue. I hated that truth, but it was still the truth.

Sano let out a quiet breath. "Just like Dad probably never planned to tell me that you were the one who's supposed to take over the business?"

I froze.

73

"I was going to come to dinner that night," he continued. "But I stopped outside the dining room when I heard him talking to you about it. He never had any intention of including me. My only question is... if he never wanted me to be a part of the family business, why did he want to keep me so badly?"

He turned back to his desk, scribbled something down, then just sat there, absently rolling his pencil across the surface.

I swallowed the knot in my throat. "I don't know why our parents do the things they do. But you know I'm here for you, right? You've always been my brother—and you always will be. And Jay, too. We aren't the same as them."

I couldn't answer his questions. I couldn't fix what had already happened. But I needed him to know he wasn't alone.

"Thanks," Sano muttered.

We sat at our desks a little longer before getting ready for bed. I should have been exhausted, but sleep didn't come easily. Then again, that wasn't unusual lately.

At some point in the night, I rolled over, half-awake. A faint sound stirred me, and through my bleary vision, I thought I saw Sano moving around. Or at least, I assumed it was him. A figure stood in the dim light, a large bag slung over their back, something else clutched in front. Were they facing me? Or the window? I couldn't tell. My mind, heavy with sleep, convinced me it was just a dream. I turned over and let the thought drift away...

The next sound I heard was an alarm.

I reached for my clock, but the ringing continued. That's when I realized—it wasn't mine. It was Sano's.

We both set alarms, just in case one of us didn't wake up. But this time, he wasn't turning his off.

I groaned. "Are you really sleeping through that noise?"

There was no response.

That was odd. Even lately, when he wasn't talking much, he'd at least mumble something back. I sat up, blinking sleep from my eyes, and turned toward his bed.

"Sano?"

The covers were pulled back. The bed was empty.

A strange unease gripped my chest. Maybe he just got up early? I shut off his alarm and walked to the bathroom—untouched. The sink was dry. No sign of use since last night.

And then it hit me.

The figure. That shadow in the night—had that really been a dream?

A cold chill crawled up my spine. My heartbeat pounded in my ears as I spun on my heel and rushed downstairs, checking everywhere.

First the living room. Empty.

The game room. Nothing.

Dining room. No sign of him.

Kitchen—

"Good morning, Kenny-kens. What's got you all fired up this early?" Jay stood at the stove, flipping something in the pan. His usual teasing smile faltered when he saw me. His expression darkened with concern. "Did something happen?"

"Have you seen Sano?" I asked, almost breathless.

"No, not yet today. Why? You haven't seen him?" He stepped closer, eyes scanning my face as realization set in.

"He wasn't in our room when I woke up."

Jay's brows furrowed. "Okay, let's not panic just yet. Maybe he got up early and is wandering around the house somewhere."

I swallowed hard. "I don't know about around the house, but… he might've gotten up early."

Even as I said it, dread pooled in my stomach. Because deep down, I already knew…

"What do you mean? You saw him earlier this morning?"

"I thought I was dreaming…" My voice trailed off. The memory of that shadowy figure came rushing back. The bag. The movement. It wasn't a dream. That was really him.

Jay opened his mouth to say something, but before he could, a loud noise echoed from the entrance hall.

"Kenneth! Jayson!"

I froze. That panicked voice—I knew it anywhere.

Mom.

Jay and I rushed toward the entrance, and there she stood, completely disheveled. She was in her work clothes, but they looked like they'd been thrown on in a hurry. Her shoes didn't even match. No makeup. Hair pulled into a messy ponytail. Her breath was ragged, like she'd been running.

"Kelly, what's wrong? Why are you here? And this early?" Jay asked, concern laced in his voice.

Her frantic eyes darted between us. "Jayson, Ken… where's your brother?"

A lump formed in my throat. "I—I don't know."

Horror washed over her face. She shook her head, placing a trembling hand over her mouth. "I can't believe it."

"Kelly?" Jay asked, his voice softer now.

She looked at him, and that's when I saw it—the tears brimming in her eyes.

"I got a message from him earlier," she admitted. "I didn't see it until I woke up. I knew something was wrong with it, but… it seems he's gone already."

Jay's patience was running thin. "What do you mean gone already?"

The words slipped out of me before I could stop them.

"He ran away."

The room fell eerily silent.

Jay's jaw tightened. "Ran away? Sano? From here?" He shook his head, still trying to wrap his mind around it. "Why would he run away? I know things haven't been easy for him, but... to just leave?"

I turned back to Mom. "What did he say to you?"

She looked at me, eyes glistening, but didn't respond right away. When she did, her voice was barely a whisper.

"He said... 'Thanks for all you've done. And thanks for telling me the truth. I'll go to where I belong now.'"

Her words sent a chill through me.

Jay exhaled sharply, running a hand down his face. "Come sit down, please." He gently guided Mom to the table at the back of the entrance hall. She collapsed into the chair just as the first tear slipped down her cheek.

"We need to check the entrance cameras," Jay said, already pulling out his phone. Mom gave a shaky nod.

We crowded around him as he opened the security app, his fingers flying over the screen as he searched for the right footage.

And as the screen loaded, I braced myself. Because whatever we were about to see... I had a feeling it would change everything.

"There doesn't seem to be anyone waiting outside," Jay muttered, rewinding the footage to the time Mom received the message.

Then we saw it.

The front door creaked open slowly, and out stepped Sano, a large bag strapped to his back, a smaller one clutched in his hand.

Time stamp: 4:03 AM. Just a few hours ago.

The three of us sat frozen, watching as he walked down the driveway, his figure shrinking into the darkness.

"Where is he going on foot?" Jay's voice was louder than he probably intended. He shifted the screen, hoping to catch a glimpse of where Sano went, but the camera's view cut off just past the main entrance.

"He really left." Mom's voice came out hollow. "This is my fault. If I hadn't said anything, he wouldn't have done this."

Before Jay could respond, a voice interrupted from the staircase.

"What's all the commotion so early in the morning?" It was Dad.

He descended the stairs, his gaze flicking between us. "Kelly? What brings you by so suddenly?" His brow furrowed when he finally noticed the expressions on our faces—shock, worry, and the unmistakable weight of uncertainty.

Jay exhaled sharply. "Sano left the house in the middle of the night."

A heavy silence settled over the room.

Dad stood frozen, his eyes wide, as if the words hadn't fully registered. "So... he's not here right now?" He glanced around, scanning the room as if expecting Sano to materialize from the shadows. Jay shook his head.

Dad turned to Mom. "Did you know about this?"

Mom's lips trembled. "He sent me a strange message early this morning. I came here as soon as I saw it." She pulled out her phone with shaky hands, showing him the message. Dad read it, his face unreadable. His gaze snapped to me and Jay.

"Did he say anything to either of you? Did you see him leave?"

My throat tightened. I opened my mouth, but no words came out. I couldn't tell him. Couldn't tell them that I had seen him—that I had noticed something strange but convinced myself it was just a dream.

"I... I didn't," I said, the weight of the half-truth sinking like a stone in my chest.

Jay sighed, rubbing his forehead. "You know how he's been lately. He hasn't been social. It was hard to get a read on him. I never thought he'd just... leave."

Dad straightened, taking a slow breath, trying to regain his composure. "Let's backtrack for a second. Has anyone tried calling him?"

Mom shook her head. "His phone's off. Goes straight to voicemail."

Dad pinched the bridge of his nose, a deep sigh escaping his lips. Then, with a resigned look, he muttered, "What about Sasha?"

The air in the room shifted.

Because we all knew. We all knew exactly where he had gone.

"I tried her too," Mom said, her voice barely above a whisper. "She didn't answer." A new level of concern darkened Mom's face, her eyes wide with a growing dread.

Jay shifted, eyes narrowing in thought. "Should we call the police?"

"Let me try Sasha one more time," Dad said, already pulling out his phone.

Jay's frustration flared. "Are you sure we should just wait? He's only thirteen. He left in the middle of the night—on foot. Who knows if he even made it to her house?" His worry was rising to Mom's level.

I glanced at her. She had her forehead pressed into her hands, her shoulders trembling.

Dad exhaled sharply, rubbing his jaw. "There is no telling what'll happen this time if we get the police involved. If things go south, he may not be able to come back to either of us."

Mom slowly lifted her head, her eyes locking with his. For a long moment, they just stared at each other, the weight of unspoken words hanging between them. Finally, Dad turned away, striding toward his office.

"Give me twenty minutes," he said over his shoulder. "I'll find out where he is."

Jay didn't hesitate. His went right back to his phone. "Maybe I should call Chris," he muttered under his breath.

Mom suddenly pushed herself up from her chair, her movement unsteady. She nearly collided with Jay. "Maybe I should just go to Sasha's. I came here when I should've gone straight there—to see if he made it there okay."

"Aunt Kelly, please," Jay caught her by the shoulders, steadying her as she swayed. "You need to calm down."

Her hands trembled as she looked at him, her voice barely a whisper. "I thought it was better for him to know the truth. But for him to leave like this—without telling anyone—and that message he sent me... I thought we were okay, but now, I'm..." She swallowed hard, her eyes glassy with guilt. "If anything happens to him, it's my fault."

Jay's voice softened with reassurance, though it didn't hide the worry in his eyes. "Papa Masy will figure it out. He always gets answers when he needs them."

"I just wish I had known what was going on," I murmured, my voice barely audible. Both of them turned toward me.

"I didn't see it," I admitted. "I didn't know he was planning this. But looking back, I think he was trying to tell me. He's been so different lately, and this morning—when I saw him... I didn't realize what he was doing. Maybe if I had, I could've stopped him."

My gaze wandered toward the door, my mind racing. How far had he made it by now? Sano had never gone to Sasha's before. Mom gave us the address, but could he even get there on his own? The uncertainty gnawed at me.

"Sano was always reserved," Mom said softly, her voice trembling. "I don't think any of us realized how much he was holding in. How hard he was taking everything." She reached out, her hand landing on my shoulder with a gentle, shaky touch. "It's not your fault, sweetie. None of us knew."

Mom's chest rose and fell with a deep breath as she tried to steady herself. "I'm just glad we noticed before too much time passed. Let's wait and see what Kenneth finds out," she said, though the words felt heavy in the silence that followed as the three of us waited.

Chapter 9

"He showed up at Sasha's house a few hours ago. He's safe."

Dad's voice broke the tense silence as he rejoined us in the entrance room. The wait had felt like forever. A collective sigh of relief filled the space.

"But," he continued, rubbing the back of his neck, "I couldn't get much out of her. She insisted on talking to him first—then she'd discuss with me what happens next."

"Are you going to let him stay there?" I asked.

Dad exhaled slowly. "As much as I want him back... I don't think I'll get him back this time." His words were heavy and hit even heavier.

"Kelly, can I have a word with you?" he asked.

Mom hesitated, then nodded. Before following him, she turned to me, giving me a hug and a kiss on the cheek. "I'll see you again before I leave."

As she and Dad walked off, Jay sank back into his chair, running a hand down his face.

"Kenny-kens," he sighed, "I'm just relieved he's safe. But... I have some blame in this too."

I frowned. "Why? You didn't do anything."

"That's kind of the problem." He stared at the floor. "I suggested we give him space. Maybe he got too much of it."

Jay had been trying so hard to hold everything together—to keep us from falling apart. Seeing him like this felt wrong. I never wanted to see him broken again.

"Do you think we'll see him again?" I asked quietly.

"I hope so. But if Papa Masy's right... I don't know if it'll be anytime soon."

I hesitated. "What did Dad mean when he said Sano wouldn't be able to stay with us or Mom if we called the police?"

Jay didn't answer. His gaze stayed fixed on the glass table, his reflection staring back at him.

That silence told me everything.

"So even after Sano runs away, you still won't tell me anything?"

He let out a slow breath. "I've been trying to piece it together myself. I only know bits and pieces—not the full story. And until I do..." He finally looked up at me. "Now's not the time to explain it."

"When will it be time?" I demanded. "When years pass and we still haven't seen or heard from him? What if I left too? Would you explain it to me then?"

Jay quickly grabbed hold of my arm.

"You can be angry, upset—whatever you need to be. Just don't joke like that," he said, his voice tight. "I don't think anyone would recover if you left too. Don't make us worry more than we already are." His fingers pressed into my skin, as if afraid I'd slip away right then and there.

I exhaled, my anger fading into something heavier. "I'm sorry. I'm not planning on leaving."

I never wanted to hurt Jay—never wanted to make him feel worse than he already did. I had just lost one brother. I didn't want him to feel like he was losing another.

I didn't go to school that day. No one did much of anything. The house felt different—quieter, like the weight of Sano's absence had settled into the walls.

By nightfall, Dad finally heard back from Sano's mom. She told him Sano didn't want to leave. He had no intention of coming back. She apologized, but she wasn't going to force him. If he wanted to stay, she would let him.

And just like that, I knew. Yesterday was the last time I'd ever see him.

He regretted not being with his mother from the start. Now that he'd gone through the trouble of finding her, there was no way he was leaving her again.

Mom stayed home all day, waiting for news. She barely moved from the couch, staring blankly at the TV—though I doubted she was actually watching it.

I sat down beside her.

"Are you okay?" she asked, wrapping an arm around my shoulders.

I hesitated before asking, "Are you?"

She let out a long breath. "I didn't want this to happen. I didn't even consider it a possibility. But… a part of me feels like maybe this is for the better. He wasn't able to be with his real mother before, but now he is. I just wish it didn't have to happen this way."

I glanced up at her. "Do you regret pretending to be his mom?"

She didn't even hesitate. "No, I don't."

Her voice was steady, unwavering. "I don't regret calling him my son. If he could accept both of us, I'd be happy. But I know now—I don't have a place in his life anymore." There was sadness in her voice, but also acceptance.

Sano had already moved on.

"I think it's about time I head out," she said softly.

"You can't stay a little longer?" I hadn't meant to say it out loud, but I didn't want her to leave just yet.

She gave me a small, sad smile and rested a hand gently on my head. "I'm sorry, sweetie. I can't stay here. This house… it's not mine anymore." She took a deep breath, as if steadying herself. "But remember, you can always see me. Anytime. If there's somewhere you want to go, or if you just want to stop by, you just say the word. But me staying here? That's not an option."

I knew I wasn't hiding how much I hated watching her leave. It must have been written all over my face. She pulled me into a hug—warm and steady, like she was trying to pass some of that strength to me. I closed my eyes, trying to let it sink in, trying not to let my emotions make this harder for her than it already was.

"Next Saturday is your special day, right?" she said, pulling back just enough to look at me. "How about we make it a full day, just you and me? Jayson can come too if you want."

Next week, I would turn thirteen. At first, I had been looking forward to finally being a teenager like Sano. But now, without him here to show off to, the excitement had already faded.

"Okay," I said, forcing a smile to assure her I was happy with the idea.

"Alright, it's settled. I'll see you then."

She stood and gathered her things, and I walked with her to the door. When she stepped outside, I stayed behind, watching as the door closed between us.

A long exhale behind me made me turn. Jay was there, hands in his pockets, watching me.

"Your mom's doing her best to keep it together," he said. "Most people wouldn't be able to handle losing a husband and their kids as well as this."

I wanted to say something, but the sound of approaching footsteps stopped me.

"Ken, mind if I have a word with you?" Dad had appeared in the hall next to Jay.

"I'll see how they're doing with dinner," Jay said, giving me a brief glance before heading toward the kitchen.

84

Dad stepped closer. "I'm sorry this had to happen," he said. "This is one case I don't think I'll be able to win. But that doesn't mean I'll just let it be. What it does mean is… you may be on your own for a while."

Mom was gone. Sano was gone. I really would be on my own now.

"With everything that's happened, I've realized I haven't done enough to keep you both safe under my roof," Dad said, his voice heavy with resolve. "I'm installing a better security system—one that covers every inch of this property. And I'm also thinking about homeschooling you."

"Homeschooled?" The words hit me like a punch to the chest. "Why?"

"I have a lot to set right around here. Too much has happened outside of my control, and I can't let anything happen to you too. This way, I'll always know where you are. I'll be able to reach you easily."

"You don't have to keep an eye on me. I'm not going anywhere." But as I said it, I already felt my connection to the outside world slipping through my fingers.

Dad's expression didn't waver. "I just want to make sure you're safe, Ken. I should have been paying more attention. I have to do better."

"Keeping me locked up here won't make anything better," I shot back. "Why are you trying so hard to keep me in and shut the rest of the world out?"

"I only want what's best for you," he said, his tone clipped. "And everything you need is right here. It'll be a lot harder to keep you on the right path if you start getting too involved out there."

"So that's what this is really about?" I let out a bitter laugh. "You just want to make sure I follow the path you've laid out for me? I don't get a say in what I do?" My fists clenched at my sides. "This is all for your business, isn't it? What if I want something different? What if locking me up in here just makes me end up like Sano? You can't shield me forever."

His eyes darkened. "That kind of thinking is exactly why this is for the best."

"And your kind of thinking," I snapped, my anger boiling over, "is why I don't have my brother or my mother here anymore!"

The words hung in the air like a slap. I had never talked back to him like that before.

I turned on my heel and walked away before he could say another word.

Watching Mom and Sano leave today had already changed the way I saw everything.

Especially him.

Chapter 10

Days passed and weeks went by. Hope faded with each one.

Sano wasn't coming back.

I only saw Mom a couple of times a week. Jay and I did almost everything together—he took me to visit her and anywhere else I wanted to go. Dad and I only spoke when necessary.

Not much else had changed. Except for the car.

Lately, a sleek gray Lexus had been parked outside more and more often. I rarely saw who it belonged to, but I knew Dad always made a point to greet the woman driving it at the door.

Now, from the balcony, I watched as it pulled up the driveway again. I heard Dad heading downstairs just as the driver stepped out. But this time, she wasn't alone. A young girl followed her—one who looked strangely familiar.

"Ken," Dad called up to me.

I made my way down the stairs, unsure of what to expect.

"Well, hello, little Kenneth." The woman was the first to greet me, her voice smooth and practiced. "So nice to see you again."

I studied her properly for the first time. Long, thick black hair. She looked only a few years older than Jay. A fitted red dress under a tailored black jacket with gray trim. No logos that I could see, but the quality screamed high-end.

She spoke to me like we knew each other. But I'd never seen her up close before.

I had seen the girl beside her, though. She stood there, hands clasped in front of her, staring at me. I recognized her, just not from here.

"I'm sure you remember Jenny," Dad said. "You met at the New Year's party."

"Hi," she said softly. There was hesitation in her voice, like she wasn't sure how to act around me. But at least she spoke first.

"Jenny will be with us for a couple of hours," Dad continued. "Why don't you keep her company until she leaves?"

I looked at him, then at her. She smiled at the idea, as if she was actually looking forward to it.

Without another word, Dad and the woman disappeared into his office, leaving me standing there with Jenny.

"Kenneth?" she said hesitantly.

Hearing my full name—her waiting for me to answer and not my dad—felt strange.

"You can just call me Ken," I told her.

"Ken? What about Kenny? I like that name too."

Most people stuck with Ken. Jay was the only one who liked playing around with my name. I studied the girl as she did the same to me.

"Uh, sure," I said.

Her face lit up like I'd just given her the best news ever. Then, without warning, she launched herself at me, grabbing onto my arm.

"It's been so long since we last saw each other! What do you want to do today?" she asked, beaming.

She was still clinging to my arm. I wasn't sure how to react to how... close she was. It was Saturday. Now that Sano was gone, I didn't do much besides study.

"I didn't have anything planned," I admitted, shifting slightly to put some space between us. She still didn't let go.

"Then let's figure something out together!" she said brightly, finally releasing me as she turned to take in the grand entryway.

"Your house is so big. I bet you could get lost in here," she said, spinning back to face me.

She wasn't wrong. One time, Sano and I had hidden from Jay after pulling a prank on him. He didn't find us until late at night, when we finally crawled out of the storage room in the back.

"Do you have games? I bet you have a game room somewhere, right?"

"We do, actually." I pointed down the hall. "But I doubt you'd want to play anything I have."

"I'm willing to try!" she said, determined.

Before I could say anything else, she grabbed my hand and pulled me along in the direction I pointed.

"Wow, this is so cool!" she gasped as we stepped inside.

The room was packed with entertainment—video games, board games, and PC setups. A large flat-screen TV hung on the wall, with a long shelf underneath holding consoles and stacks of games. A black couch sat in front of it. Across the room, two computers lined a desk, and an old shelving unit held stacks of board games we played now and then.

"Oh, what's that? I think I know this game!" She rushed to the video game shelf and grabbed a racing game.

"Are you sure you want to play that?" I asked, raising an eyebrow.

I didn't know a lot of girls, but I was pretty sure most of them wouldn't want to sit around playing video games.

"You said you had nothing else to do, right? So, playing this should be fine," she said, staring me down.

I was starting to remember the last time we met. She was just like this then, too. At first, she seemed quiet—maybe even a little scared—but I think she was just nervous. Once she got comfortable, all that hesitation disappeared. She really seemed like she wanted to be my friend.

I went ahead and loaded the game, handing her one of the wireless controllers.

"Oh wow, you can play without it being plugged in? I've never used a controller like this before."

"It works the same as a regular controller, just without the cord," I explained. She really must not play games much if she's never used a wireless one before.

She wasn't all that bad. Everything seemed to amaze her, which made me wonder—what kind of place is she from? And how does she know that woman? She looks too young to be her daughter. But maybe she is...

"Could you show me how to play?" Jenny turned to me expectantly.

"I thought you said you knew this game?"

"I've seen it, but I haven't actually played it," she admitted. The game finished loading, and she suddenly panicked.

"Relax, the game hasn't started yet. It's not that hard to figure out," I reassured her. "You'll mostly use these buttons." I pointed out the controls, and she settled down.

I had her pick a character and a car, then selected a map. The race started. Not even five seconds in, she drove straight off the track.

I couldn't help but laugh. Even Mom didn't do that the last time I convinced her to play.

"I didn't think it would be this hard," she muttered, gripping the controller like it might slip away from her.

She was dead last, and there was no way she'd catch up. But she didn't give up. Somehow, by the end, she managed to climb out of last place.

"You did pretty good, considering how you started," I said.

90

"This won't do. I'm not a failure!" she declared, determination blazing in her eyes. "I'll keep trying until I win! I want to play again."

"You really think you can beat me?" I smirked.

"I know I can, if I keep trying."

"Alright, alright." I let the next match start.

It had been a while since I played, anyway. With everything going on, I hadn't really felt up to it.

"Kenny-Kens, are you in here?" Jay's voice rang out as he stepped into the room.

"Oh, I didn't know you had company," he added, his gaze landing on Jenny beside me. His smile widened, but something about it felt... off. Like he wasn't just being his usual friendly self.

"Jay, this is Jenny. Jenny, that's Jay."

"Hi..." she said, suddenly nervous again.

"Well, hello there, Jenny." Jay smirked. "Aren't you just the cutest little kitten? But tell me, where did you come from?"

"I came with... Jocelyn. She brought me here," Jenny replied.

Jay's expression shifted. "Jocelyn?"

"The lady that's been coming here for Dad," I clarified.

"Oh, right, right." He waved it off like he should've known. "Well, don't let me interrupt. You two seem to be having fun." He eyed the controllers in our hands, but the glint in his eyes told me he was completely misunderstanding the situation.

Before I could correct him, my phone buzzed with a message.

"You seem to be popular today, Kenny-Kens," Jay teased.

My amusement faded when I saw the name on the screen.

"It's from Sano."

Jay's head snapped toward me. "Our lovely little Sano? He messaged you?" His voice was full of shock. None of us had heard from Sano since he left.

91

"Is everything okay?" Jenny asked, confused by the sudden shift in atmosphere.

"Uh… yeah, it's fine." I kept my eyes on the message.

—*Sorry for leaving. But I had to.*

That was it. After more than a month of silence, this was all he had to say.

"He must be settled in now if he's reaching out," Jay mused.

I wasn't so sure. The message was short—too short. And it didn't sound like he was planning to come back. Maybe he liked it there with his mom. Maybe this was him saying goodbye.

Jenny glanced between Jay and me, then at my phone.

"Did this person move away or something?"

"Yeah…" There was no point in hiding it. We'd already had gotten used to him being gone.

"I'm sorry," she said, her voice softer now. "He must be really important to you for you to get so sadden by this… You looked so happy playing the game. I want you to smile like that again. So please… feel better soon." She was trying to comfort me. I didn't know her well, but it was kind of nice.

And then—

She dropped the controller, launched herself at me, and kissed me.

"Oh, my sweet sugar," Jay gasped, as if witnessing the most dramatic romance in history.

"What was that for?" I asked, scooting away.

Jenny tilted her head. "My mom always says that showing affection makes people happy, so I was trying to make you happy and not sad anymore. Did it not work?" Her expression fell slightly, like she was genuinely disappointed.

I was too stunned to answer. My first kiss—just stolen by a stranger.

"Should I try again?" She leaned forward.

"No, that's okay." I quickly put my hands up, blocking her path. Then I glanced at Jay, hoping for some kind of backup.

Instead, he just smirked. "Well, I guess I'll head out for now. If you need me, you can page me—I'm on line three. Anna and Rachel are on line two if you want snacks or anything." And with that, he strolled out.

Wait. What? That was it? I expected him to stick around, maybe even interrogate Jenny or launch another investigation, but instead, he just... left?

"Oh wow, you guys have an intercom system too?" Jenny got up, walking over to the desk with the computers and pager. She leaned in, examining it like it was the most fascinating thing in the world.

I watched her, trying to make sense of everything. There was something unusual about her—she was too friendly. Especially with someone she barely knew.

"You're not used to this kind of stuff, are you?" I asked, raising an eyebrow.

"Well, kind of," she said, running her fingers lightly over the desk. "We know a lot of people who have similar things, so it's always cool to see the different setups people have."

I frowned slightly. "We? Is that lady you came with your mom?"

"No, but she's with us a lot, so she takes us places. Me and my sister, that is. But my sister was busy with friends today, so she didn't come."

"Has she known my dad for a long time?"

Jenny thought for a moment. "I don't know. I think I first met him two years ago?" She returned to the couch, plopping down beside me like we'd been friends forever.

Her eyes flickered to my phone. "Did you message that person back?"

I looked down. The screen still showed Sano's message.

"…No, I didn't."

Honestly, I'd been too distracted by Jenny attacking me. But beyond that, I wasn't even sure how to respond.

Jenny smiled. "You don't have to right now, but you should. If someone left and then messaged you, that means they want to talk to you, right?" She said it so simply, like it was obvious.

And maybe… maybe she was right.

We'd all started to believe Sano was done with us—that he didn't want anything to do with us anymore. But here he was, reaching out. Saying he was sorry. That had to mean something.

Jenny was bold, but she didn't try anything else after that first attack. We ended up playing different games the whole time she was here. I still kept a little space between us—just in case she decided to show affection again.

She looked genuinely sad when it was time to leave, promising she'd come by again. If she was always around that Jocelyn lady, I figured I'd probably see her again sooner or later.

After they left, my dad glanced at me. "Did you two enjoy yourselves?"

"We just played games the whole time," I shrugged.

He chuckled. "Jenny's a sweet girl. I don't think I've ever seen her touch a game before, but she did for you."

I wasn't surprised. From the way she struggled with the controller, it was obvious she wasn't around people who played much. But still, it was the first thing she said she wanted to do. Was she trying to impress me?

"You could use a girl like her," Dad went on. "If you and Jenny get to know each other better, I could see her being a good wife in the future."

I nearly choked. "Wife? Her? With me?"

He gave me a knowing look. "Yes, wife. You don't think so?"

"Dad, I'm thirteen. Not exactly something I'm thinking about right now."

"I know, I know," he said, waving it off. "But it's always good to know your options."

I frowned. "Options? Are you, like... looking for me a wife or something?"

"That's not the case at the moment," he said smoothly. "But within the coming years, it would be nice to know the possible new family member."

His tone made it sound like he'd already mapped out my future, like this was just another step in some grand plan. A wife, a family—everything planned before I even knew what I wanted. He hadn't even told me what he planned to do with me, so why was he already thinking about marriage?

What if I don't even want to get married? Was that an option in his plans?

"It's just something to keep in the back of your mind," he added before walking off.

Ever since Jocelyn started coming around, Dad had been different. I wasn't sure how yet, but something about her had shifted his focus.

The thought reminded me of the message from Sano—the one I still hadn't replied to. I felt bad for waiting so long, but he was the one who disappeared for a month. We'd all been waiting to hear from him, and when he finally reached out, all he said was sorry for leaving.

It was better than nothing, I supposed. I had almost come to terms with never hearing from him again. So I better take what I can get.

No matter what the truth may be, I still consider him my brother—my whole brother. That's something that will never change.

And with everything else constantly shifting around me, I didn't want Sano to think that no one here cared about him anymore.

So, with that thought pressing down on me, I pulled out my phone and typed a reply:

—*It's okay. At least one of us managed to get free.*

Chapter 11

Living within the walls of our mansion makes me wonder about the lives of people who don't live like this. I imagine they go out whenever they want, without waiting for permission or needing someone to take them everywhere. They don't have to plan around the maid's schedule just to get their laundry done.

We live outside the city, surrounded by trees and long, open roads. I still don't know how Sano managed to leave without getting lost. He must have planned it carefully to make it all the way to his mother's house on his own.

"Kenny-Kens." I heard Jay's voice coming down the hall before he reached my room. "I need to talk to you about something."

Even though it was Jay, a part of me didn't want to hear it. Nothing good ever comes after someone says they need to talk.

"What is it?" I asked, turning away from my desk. The look in his eyes told me I wasn't going to like the answer.

"It's not really a talk—more of a question. From Papa Masy," he clarified.

I frowned. "What do you mean, a question?"

"Well," Jay said, leaning against the doorframe, "he knows you've been in touch with our lovely little Sano, and he was just wondering… has Sano mentioned wanting to come back? Or visit? Or—anything? Just something where we could, you know… see him?"

I blinked. "Dad asked you to ask me all that?"

"Not in those exact words, but yeah, that's basically what he meant."

I sat back in my chair, still processing. "I didn't think he cared enough to want to know about Sano."

Jay sighed. "What do you mean? Not to play devil's advocate, but I hope you realize Papa Masy hasn't quite been himself since Sano left."

"I know he's been different. But I'm pretty sure it has more to do with that Jocelyn lady."

"Well... there's that," Jay admitted, stepping inside. "But maybe he just needs that distraction."

"Distraction?" I repeated, watching as Jay closed my door and sat on the edge of my bed.

"He talked to me a couple of times, you know," Jay said. "Losing half your family like that is really hard, even for him. Sano left from under his roof. He may not always be around, but that doesn't mean you kids don't mean the world to him."

"If that were really the case, he would've tried harder to stop Sano from leaving. Or at least brought him back."

Jay sighed. "He calls Sasha at least twice a week."

I frowned. "He does?"

"Sano still doesn't want to talk to him. I guess Sasha feels bad about all of this, so she tells him how Sano's doing—for now."

"I didn't know that." I sat back, processing the information. Dad and I don't talk much anymore, so I had no idea he'd been keeping in touch with his mother.

"He's trying not to let it get to him," Jay continued. "But that's also why he's keeping a closer eye on you. He's trying to make sure what happened with Sano doesn't happen again."

"Well, he doesn't have to monitor me. I'm not going anywhere." I scoffed.

"We didn't think Sano would, either." Jay leaned forward, resting his elbows on his knees. "You know, if you ever want to go somewhere, I can take you. We just have to let Papa Masy know where we're going and how long we'll be gone."

I rolled my eyes. "And you don't think that's a bit much? Always having to report where I'm going, for how long? If we get stuck at a red light too long, we have to call and let him know we'll be a few minutes late."

Jay exhaled heavily. "We could sit here all day arguing about how Papa Masy runs things, but if we put that aside for just a second... maybe try steering your conversations with Sano toward something meaningful—it'd go a long way. Not just for him, but for me too." He hesitated before adding, "I want to see him again, ask him how he's doing. But right now, it seems like he's only willing to talk to you."

I studied him for a moment. I think Jay wants this information more for himself than for Dad. He's upset that Sano won't talk to him, that I'm the only one he'll reach out to. Maybe it's because Sano knows I won't run back and tell Dad everything he says. Jay has our back. But at the end of the day, he still has an obligation to tell Dad certain things. And Sano knows that too.

I hadn't actually asked Sano about coming back or visiting. It didn't feel like the right time to bring him back into the life he fought to escape. But I couldn't help wondering—would there ever be another chance to see him again?

"I'll see what I can do," I told Jay. It wasn't just because Dad wanted me to—it was because we all wanted to know how Sano was really doing.

Jay grinned. "Knew you'd come around. Oh, and by the way... how are things with that cute little kitten, Jenny? She came over again yesterday, didn't she?"

"She's alright, I guess. Just... really clingy."

"I actually asked Papa Masy about her," he said, feigning innocence. "You know, out of concern—after that little display of affection she gave you."

I narrowed my eyes. "Did you tell him what she did?"

"I wanted to," he admitted. "But I figured it was harmless, and she hasn't done it again. She seems like a sweet girl, so I guess we'll see what happens. She doesn't have a lot of friends, apparently, so he thought you two could get to know each other."

I scoffed. "He also said she'd make a good wife for me." Just repeating it made my skin crawl.

Jay let out a low whistle. "Bringing that up already at your age, huh? Can't say I've seen you hanging around girls much, though. Maybe that's what he's trying to change. I tell you, Kenny-Kens, once you enter the world of women, your life will be completely different." He smirked like he was letting me in on some grand secret.

I leaned forward. "Why don't you tell me what I should know then?"

"Absolutely not." He waved off the question.

"Oh, come on. You know everything about this stuff. If I'm always stuck here, how else am I supposed to learn how to handle girls without any experience?"

"You're thirteen. I don't approve of you playing in this field just yet."

"Okay, but when I do get to the age you approve of, I should at least know what to do, right? You shouldn't let me play the game without knowing the rules." I smirked.

Jay gave me a knowing look. "It's been a while since you tried that one on me. I remember a swollen face the last time you played the game—and lost."

The memory hit me instantly—the mall incident. I groaned.

Jay chuckled. "That reminds me, I need to talk to Chris. For some reason, he still thinks we need information on the wrong person. Left me a message saying he dropped off some more intel he gathered." He shook his head. "Business must be slow for him if he's still at it. I need to tell him to drop that investigation."

"You're still getting stuff about Misa?" I asked, unable to hide my curiosity, even after all this time.

Jay sighed. "Yeah. I feel bad that we've had her investigated for this long. She's just a regular girl. Not even the one I was looking for. Let me just call him now and tell him to drop this." He headed out of my room.

"Wait." I stopped him before he reached the door. "I want to see what else he found on her."

Jay raised an eyebrow. "Are you sure you need to do that? I mean, you could just talk to Jenny. She seems normal enough."

"Jenny's different," I admitted. "But she's not normal, that's for sure. She's used to this lifestyle. Misa? She's nothing like us. She couldn't even afford a piece of jewelry she saved up for. But she still seemed happy with her life—happy with her friend, anyway."

"You mean assault demon," Jay corrected with a smirk.

"Whatever. The point is, can't I be a little curious about someone my dad doesn't know about? Someone he isn't trying to marry me off to?"

Jay let out a dramatic sigh, but his grin betrayed him. "You're putting me in a really tough spot here." Then, he narrowed his eyes at me. "Did you really think she was that cute?"

"I—well…" I hesitated, caught off guard. I wasn't sure what it was or why I cared so much. Maybe part of me still wanted to know what would've happened if I had been just a regular kid from her neighborhood. If I had gone to her school. If we had kept in touch—just so she could pay me back.

Jay checked his watch. "Your mom really picked a fine time to leave. With Papa Masy always busy, I guess that means I have to teach you the ropes." His lips curled into a mischievous grin. "Come on, let's sneak out before he notices you're gone.

The second I saw that sneaky smile and those narrowed eyes, I knew he had something planned. Jay could play the responsible parent role when he had to, but he also knew how to be a friend. If he had moved out with my mom, I really wouldn't have anyone anymore.

Summer break was coming, which meant the sun stayed out longer. So even though it was already after five, the sky was still bright. That meant my dad wouldn't be as mad about us going out—at least not as much as he would be if we stayed out after dark.

I didn't really care where Jay took me. As long as it meant I got to step outside—free from constant surveillance.

"We'd both end up sitting in Papa Masy's office if I took you too far," Jay said as he pulled into the corner bakery he'd taken me to before. "So why don't we just relax here for a bit?"

"Sneaking out and dessert before dinner? You're on a roll today, Jay." My words dripped with sarcasm. I knew he had a sweet tooth, but a bakery wasn't exactly what I had in mind for a getaway.

"Very funny," he said, rolling his eyes. "I just figured we needed somewhere close and not too public. And what better place than our peaceful little corner bakery?"

We got out of the car and walked inside. The place was quiet, with only a handful of customers scattered around. They'd be closing in about an hour, so the usual rush had already died down. Every time Jay brought me here, it was the same—never too crowded. It made me wonder why, since their pastries and cakes were actually really good.

"Welcome! How's my favorite customer doing today?" A woman with short black hair and glasses stepped out from the back and smiled as soon as she saw Jay.

"Everything's fine as wine," Jay said, grinning as he leaned on the glass display case. "How about you, Lexi? What's the special today?"

Lexi pointed to a nearly finished two-layer chocolate cake with strawberries in the display. "We just added this to the menu earlier this week—chocolate strawberry short cake."

Jay's eyes lit up. "Ohh, Lexi, tell me you didn't come up with this after my last visit."

She smirked. "I might have pitched the idea to my bakers, and they were all for it. You were on to something—it's been selling since we put it in the case." She winked at him. "So, as a thank-you, I'm giving you both a slice—on the house. No ifs, ands, or buts about it."

She turned to me with a warm smile. "It's been a while since I've seen you here. Stop letting him hog all the good stuff and come by anytime, okay?" She pulled out the cake and held it up. "You want this here or to go?"

"Since you're *sooo* insistent, we'll have it here," Jay said dramatically, acting as if he wouldn't have ordered it anyway.

Lexi laughed, grabbing a spatula and carefully lifting two slices onto plates. She set them on a tray and handed it over.

"Silverware and napkins are to your right. Enjoy, boys." She smiled before turning to greet someone as the door behind us chimed open.

Jay picked up the tray and started walking. "Let's sit over here," he called over his shoulder.

I barely registered what he said. My attention had shifted to the newcomers—specifically, the girl who had just walked in with an older woman. She was quiet, just like she always was in class. Her hair, usually tied back in a ponytail, was down in curls today. I don't think I've ever seen her wear it like that before, but I was certain it was her.

Jay must have noticed my distraction because he leaned in and whispered, "Do you know them?" His gaze flicked toward the girl and the woman at the counter. Before I could answer, she turned and spotted me.

"Ken?" Her voice carried a note of surprise.

I wasn't expecting her to call out to me. We'd only talked a few times since the start of the semester. She mostly kept to herself, sticking to a small circle of friends.

"I didn't think anyone else knew about this bakery," she said as she walked over. It was kind of in the middle of nowhere. I was just as surprised to run into someone from school here.

"I live around here, so I've always known about this place," I told her.

Jay had already taken a seat outside, and the woman she was with was still at the counter placing an order. It was strange seeing a familiar face outside of school. I wasn't sure how to act.

"So the rumors are true then?" she asked, eyes lighting up. "You do live in that crazy big mansion around here somewhere?" She whispered it like it was some closely guarded secret.

"After living there all your life, it doesn't seem that big anymore." I lowered my voice to match hers.

"That's so cool! Now I get why you always look so nice. You must be loaded to live in a place like that," she giggled.

There was something about the way she smiled—it wasn't like how other people looked at me after finding out I was rich. She didn't have that calculating look, the one that usually came with expectations or hidden motives. She just seemed... fascinated. It was a first.

Lately, I seemed to be experiencing a lot of firsts.

I didn't want to say anything that might change that look on her face, so I stayed quiet. Over her shoulder, I noticed the woman she'd come with picking up their order.

"I guess she got our stuff. We're having mother-daughter time, so I have to go," she said, giving me a little wave. "I'll see you in class!" And just like that, she was gone.

It was a short conversation, but somehow, it left me feeling...
confused. I wasn't sure why. I turned back to Jay, who had been
watching the whole time with a knowing grin.

"I must say, that was a lot easier to watch than that other time. I
don't have to call Chris again," he teased, clearly entertained.

"We have a class together. That's all," I said flatly, but the way he
smirked told me he didn't believe that for a second.

"I guess you have been taking notes," he continued as if I hadn't
said anything. "I really can go ahead and throw these away since I don't
have to worry about something like this happening again." He tossed a
folder onto the table.

"Where did that come from?" I asked, narrowing my eyes.

Jay zipped up his jacket and smirked. "Do you really think I'd
come to a bakery if I was actually that lumpy?"

I stared at him. "You had it with you this whole time?"

He just shrugged.

Curious, I grabbed the folder and flipped through the papers inside.

"I only brought this because you still seemed interested in knowing
more about her," he said, watching me. "But like I've said, there's
nothing special. She's just a regular girl." Jay leaned back in his chair.
"I think you should focus on someone you'll actually see again. Like
Jenny... or even her."

He nodded toward the mother and daughter sitting in a booth,
talking together.

"We're all curious about the people who pass through our lives,"
Jay said. "But for someone like you, it'd make more sense to be
interested in someone closer. This girl lives so far away—the odds of
you running into her again are slim to none. And even if you did, after
the way things went last time, I doubt she'd want to see you."

I flipped to the last page of the report and frowned. "What's this?"

"Oh, that's from the new report Chris dropped in the mailbox today. What does it say?"

I skimmed the text, then looked up. "Her parents put in applications to work for my dad's company."

Jay's eyebrows shot up. "Really? What is Chris doing looking into her parents? I swear, sometimes he does way too much."

"Or maybe he was just trying to let us know she might be around more than we thought," I said, setting the folder down.

Jay narrowed his eyes. "And what exactly are you implying?"

"Well, if her parents are applying for jobs at my dad's company, they'd have to move out here if they got hired, right? The only branch in this area is near us, and I doubt they'd make a two-hour commute every day."

Jay let out a groan. "I really don't like where this is going."

"What's the problem?" I asked. "Didn't you just say the odds of meeting again were highly unlikely? Looks like those odds just got a whole lot better."

"That's one—if either of them even get hired. You know how tough the hiring process is. And two, I really think you should just forget about this and move on. Maybe consider some other options."

"Why are you getting so serious? I told you—I'm just curious. It's not like I'm looking into some marriage deal like my dad is."

Jay stabbed his fork into his cake and shot me a look. "I'm not saying you are, but this girl probably doesn't even remember you. You kept telling me to hold off on dropping the investigation, and for what? Are you going to have me drive you to her house? Because I'm telling you now, when Papa Masy asks about the restraining order they slap on you, I will not be backing you up."

I rolled my eyes. "You're overthinking it, Jay. I'm not trying to do anything like that. Haven't you ever been curious about someone you

106

met? Weren't you the one who told me, 'Don't live life wondering what if'?"

I didn't give him time to reply before I kept going.

"I'm not saying we should go searching the whole city, but can't I at least wonder about the person I made feel bad, and almost died shortly after? Maybe if her parents get hired and they move out here, I'll get the chance to apologize. There aren't that many schools around—there's a chance we could end up at the same one."

Jay leaned back in his chair, exhaling through his nose. "Look, Kenny-Kens, you're thirteen now, and you're growing up. I get it—you want to experience more. When I was your age, I wasn't as caged in as you are. I had a lot more freedom, but because of that, I got into trouble—a lot of trouble. You might not think it now, but sticking to the routine we've got here? It's probably better for you."

I sighed and stared out into the parking lot. "Once again, you're really starting to sound like my dad."

I'd been counting on Jay to be on my side, but the more we talked, the more he started sounding like him. Dad was always telling me how different life outside our walls was—how I shouldn't get involved. But they couldn't seriously expect me to stay in that mansion forever.

Jay studied me for a moment, then let out a sigh. "With that look on your face, you really remind me of Kelly."

I frowned. "What look?"

"That 'I'm stuck here' look. She used to make that same face whenever she talked to Papa Masy about wanting to do something, and he'd say he had work to do." Jay shook his head. "I guess it runs in our side of the family—to be free spirits, to want to have fun. But your dad... he was different. He always wanted to stay in. And every time he did, she'd have that same expression."

I hesitated. "Did that happen a lot?"

107

Jay nodded. "It was one of the reasons things were hard for her there. They were just... too different. And you? You definitely have her spirit." He leaned forward, elbows on the table. "I don't want you to feel caged like she did. But, Kenny... you're still only thirteen. My hands are tied on this."

"I know," I muttered.

I was always being reminded that I was too young. Too young to do things, too young to make my own choices. I just wondered—how old did I have to be before I could actually do something without it coming with a lecture?

"Bye, Ken."

I turned and saw the girl walking out with her mother. She waved as she passed by.

Jay, still working on his cake, smirked. "I think she's more than just some girl in your class."

"I'm not even sure of her name. I think it's Lacey or something."

"Well, Lacey sure knows your name. And it's not like you to forget things. Seems like you should start remembering her."

I glanced down at the papers on Misa. "So, it's okay to remember Lacey, but not this one?"

Jay sighed, setting his fork down. "Let me put it this way—I'm more willing to turn a blind eye to Lacey than I am to this situation. So far, no one's been hurt, she looks innocent enough, and you see her every day. I still think it's too soon for you to be worrying about girls, but everyone needs a friend. As long as you're not sneaking in past curfew, I think this one's alright."

He glanced toward the parking lot, where Lacey and her mom were getting into a red car. As they backed out, I noticed Lacey looking over at me again.

"Now that I think about it, she's always looking in my direction during class. I just never thought much of it."

Jay shrugged. "Maybe now's the time to think on it. Summer vacation's coming up. It wouldn't be bad to have a friend around. This is our first summer without our lovely little Sano. It's going to be tough as it is."

I almost forgot—this summer would be different. Sano hasn't mentioned school or his summer plans at all. Part of me doesn't want to ask in case it's still a sensitive subject. But another part really wants to know if he'll just turn into another name on paper—someone I'll never cross paths with again.

Chapter 12

Jay was completely against the idea of me wanting to get to know that Misa girl. But the second he saw Lacey at the bakery, he had "*a good feeling about that one*." So I listened to him and talked to her.

It's been a few weeks now. Even after school ended, she still makes sure to message me and keep in touch. She even asked if we could hang out, but I'm not sure how my dad would feel about me going out with a girl he's never met.

"Since I put you up to this one, I'm giving you the okay to use me as your reason to be out," Jay said after quietly shutting my bedroom door. My dad was home, so he didn't want him hearing his master plans.

"I wouldn't even know where to go," I admitted. I rarely did things that didn't involve family. Coming up with somewhere to go with someone from school—a girl at that—felt like uncharted territory. I looked at Jay, who'd been keeping an eye on me these past few weeks, making sure Lacey was someone I should befriend.

"Well," he mused, settling onto my bed, "I think you should keep it simple. Let's see—young teens on summer break. One of them isn't exactly able to do much without it going noticed." He smirked, obviously referring to me.

I just sat at my desk, watching him tap his cheek in thought. "What did you do when you were my age?" Maybe his experience could give me some ideas.

"Oh, me?" He laughed. "When I was thirteen, my friend and I hung out a lot with his older brother, who was a senior. We'd stay out late and sometimes snuck into R-rated movies with them." He shook his head, remembering.

"But we got caught after one bad incident where I *accidentally* drank some of his brother's alcohol stash and went to the movies completely drunk. We ended up getting kicked out, but they didn't find out about me. My mother did, though. Needless to say, I started getting monitored after that."

"So you were out hanging with high schoolers, and I can't even hang out with someone my age?"

Jay grinned. "Yeah, well, although we had fun, I really don't recommend that route. But something else we did was go to the amusement park a lot." He paused, thinking. "None of them are close enough to here, though... Oh! But there's a fair in town next weekend. I'll volunteer to chaperone!" He raised his hand like he was volunteering for something important.

"And what do we tell my dad?"

"You leave Papa Masy to me. You'll be out for one afternoon—he'll hardly notice. Plus, next weekend, I think he's off, which means he'll most likely be with Jocelyn again."

"You don't think Jenny will come over, do you? She's been showing up more with her."

"I'll tell Papa Masy we'll be out for the day. That should keep you in the clear."

"Good." I let out a relieved breath.

"Does Jenny really bother you that much?"

"It's not that exactly. She's just... tiring."

Jay chuckled. "She does seem like a handful. And Papa Masy really likes her. I don't know her relation to Jocelyn, but she loves her too, so she's definitely not going anywhere anytime soon."

"I see that. After he mentioned her being a good wife for me, I think he wants to keep her around for that purpose."

Jay smirked. "Well, maybe if you show him you have other options…"

I narrowed my eyes. "You sure change your mind fast about not wanting me to talk to girls."

"Yeah, yeah, I know—I told you to wait. It's just so hard for me, being both a friend and something of a guardian. It's a constant battle." He sighed, then motioned toward the window. "But you know what? When you get the chance, take it. Kelly would kill me if she heard me saying this, but I hate that you're always stuck here. You should be out there, enjoying your youth." He looked back to me.

"Not exactly like I did," he added with a laugh, "but still enjoying yourself. So if someone's asking you out somewhere, I say go for it. And the fact that it's a girl who probably has a crush on you? That stays between you and me." He grinned. I couldn't help but smile, even though I was still nervous about all this.

When Jay was my age, he was always out having fun. He was super popular and even almost made it as an actor after auditioning for a role in college. But after his big breakup with his ex, Amy, he gave it all up.

Now he's here, looking after me—the one who can't even leave the house without getting interrogated. Maybe he's right. Maybe I should take chances when I get them. Besides, Lacey isn't nearly as tiring as Jenny. Hanging out with her shouldn't be that bad. My only real question is... why does she want to talk to me anyway?

I've never been to this fair Jay is taking us to, but Lacey has. She's been here before and is excited to go again. It's supposed to be the biggest one in town—something people look forward to every year.

I was worried her parents wouldn't actually let her go, but after they met Jay and talked for a bit, they practically pushed her out the door. No one seems to be able to say no to him. Can't say the same for Dad though.

Jay told him he wanted to go to the fair this year and that we were going. Dad said no at first—said it was too public, too unpredictable, too much could go wrong. But Jay reassured him it would be fine. He just left out the part about Lacey coming with us.

Now the three of us are on our way, and surprisingly, it's not as awkward as I thought it would be.

"I can't believe you've lived here your whole life and have never been." Lacey shook her head, still surprised.

"We were never really big on these kinds of events." I shrugged. "But I'm looking forward to seeing what it's like."

Telling her my days mostly consist of studying in my room and occasionally stepping outside into the backyard didn't seem like a great conversation starter.

We both sat in the back seat, and I could see the excitement on her face. She had her hair down and curly again. She seems like a different person outside of class.

At school, she's quiet, keeps to herself, and only speaks when spoken to. But now? She talks a lot, and seems more energetic. I didn't notice at first, but now that she's smiling more, I realize she has dimples. And braces.

"Oh! It's up ahead!" She pointed.

I looked up just as we neared the fairgrounds. The first thing I saw was the Ferris wheel, towering over everything, seemingly placed right in the center of all the action. Even from this distance, I could see the crowds. The place was packed. I wasn't even sure Jay would find a parking spot. He drove around for a while before finally pulling into a space toward the back.

"A little further than I wanted, but it's a full house, I see." Jay turned off the engine.

Lacey walked around to our side as we all got out, the buzz of the fair already filling the air.

"You're both under my care, and I gave Lacey's parents my word I'd bring her back in one piece. So stick with me, and we'll get this party started," Jay said as we walked toward the entrance.

He was tall and thin, but I once saw him carry someone bigger than him after they sprained their ankle. That was enough proof that I never had to worry when he took me anywhere. Lacey didn't seem to mind either.

"It's tradition to ride the Ferris wheel before we leave. I hope you don't mind being ridiculously high up in the air," Lacey said, eyes bright with excitement.

"I've never been on a Ferris wheel, so that should be fun."

"Wait—you've never been on a Ferris wheel?" She stared at me, then laughed. "Do you live under a rock?"

I hesitated. If only she knew. Compared to what she's probably done in her life, I might as well be living under a rock.

She must've noticed my pause because she softened. "Well, you did say you don't go to these kinds of events, so I guess it makes sense."

I spotted something that caught my attention and pointed toward it. "I think I want to check that out first."

A group of people was walking into an oddly shaped building that looked like a UFO.

"Oh, that's the Flying Saucer!" Lacey grinned. "It spins really fast, and you kind of stick to the walls. It feels like you're floating. It's super fun."

"I'm up for it if you both are," Jay said.

"You're going to ride too?" I asked.

Jay scoffed. "What, you thought I was just going to let you two have all the fun? Have we met before? I don't sit back for anything."

"We can all ride together. I don't mind," Lacey added.

114

"First, we need tickets. Let me grab some so we can ride as much as we want." Jay spotted the ticket counter and walked ahead. Lacey and I followed behind.

I glanced around, taking in the buzzing atmosphere. Families walked past us, groups of friends laughed together, and vendors called out their latest deals. A little kid ran by, his sleeve rolled up to show off a fresh airbrush tattoo. I'd only ever seen those done on TV. Now, everything around me—all of it—felt like a scene I was stepping into for the first time. When I looked back, I caught Lacey watching me.

"Thanks for inviting me today," she said.

"Well, you said you wanted to hang out, and I heard the fair was in town. Figured it was time to give this place a try," I shrugged.

Even though it was Jay's idea, I didn't think he'd mind if I took credit for it.

Lacey laughed. "You must have read my mind because I was just thinking about how I wanted to come here when you brought it up that day."

I couldn't help but smile. She looked so happy every time she laughed.

Jay turned to us. "I'm getting the unlimited passes, so you'll be able to ride as much as you want."

Lacey's excitement faltered a little. "Oh, my mom gave me money, but I don't think I'll have enough for that and games and food."

Jay waved a dismissive hand. "Oh, Lacey dear, I hope you didn't think we'd let you pay. When you're in our company, you don't have to worry about a thing." He handed her a wristband with a wink. "Save your money for another party."

Her dimples flashed as she beamed. "Wow, thank you so much! You guys are awesome!"

Once again, Jay had effortlessly charmed someone. He did it so naturally, I wasn't even sure he realized when he was doing it.

I grinned at Lacey. "This just means we can ride whatever you want. I hope you like rides, because I'm ready to try them all."

She smirked. "I don't know who you think I am, but I'm a girl who loves rides. So you better keep your word."

Jay handed me my pass, and we headed for the first ride I'd picked—the Flying Saucer.

We arrived just as a group of people was stumbling off, laughing. Well, most of them. Two girls clutched their stomachs, looking like they regretted every decision that led them there.

Lacey leaned toward me. "It goes super fast, so don't throw up, okay?"

I had an idea of what to expect, but stepping inside was different than I imagined. The space was smaller than it looked from the outside.

"Stand here," Lacey said, pressing her back against one of the panel-like walls.

I moved to the panel beside hers, mirroring her stance, and Jay took the one next to me.

"Welcome aboard the spaceship, everyone," a man sitting in the middle announced. "You guys ready to have some fun?"

The crowd erupted in cheers.

"Keep your feet on the ground, and enjoy the ride!"

At first, I couldn't tell if anything was actually happening—just a loud mechanical hum as the ride powered up. Then, slowly, I felt it start to move. Nothing too extreme at first. But then, it sped up.

A force pushed me harder against the wall, making it impossible to move. Laughter and screams filled the air. Next to me, Lacey was laughing too. The rush was unlike anything I'd ever felt before. Then, just like she said, the panel I was leaning against lifted, making me feel weightless.

The ride spun faster and faster until a horn-like sound blared, signaling it was slowing down.

"Thanks for riding the Saucer! Please refrain from moving until we've come to a complete stop," the announcer called out.

The pressure eased, and I could move again.

Lacey turned to me, eyes bright. "So? How'd you like that?"

"That was fun! I've never done anything like this before." I turned to Jay. "How about you?"

Jay was busy fixing his hair. "It's been a while for me, but that was fun. Not so much for my hair, though." He ran a hand through it, smoothing it back.

Lacey winced. "I guess I should've warned you."

Jay waved her off. "Oh, please. No amount of wind can ruin this look."

We stepped out into the fairground, and I took a moment to look around. There was so much I hadn't seen yet. I needed to think faster before Lacey beat me to another question.

"What do you want to do next?" she asked, right on cue.

I scanned the area, trying to pick something quickly. "What's this over here?"

We walked toward a booth stacked with bottles. Someone was already playing, tossing small rings at them.

Lacey smirked. "Let me guess—you've never played a ring toss either?"

I hesitated.

"Yeah, that's what I thought." She laughed. "It's simple—well, not really, you have to toss the ring onto the bottle to win a prize. But it's super hard. I've never won this game."

I watched as the person ahead of us tossed a ring. They missed every time. One got close, but it bounced off the bottle's neck and fell to the ground.

"Why don't you show them how it's done, Kenny-Kens?" Jay nudged me. "A bucket, please."

117

The booth attendant handed him a bucket of rings, which Jay passed to me. I took it, just looking at the rings inside.

"What? Don't tell me you don't think you can do it," Jay smirked.

It had been a while since I was last put on the spot like this. If I remembered right, the last time was at the mall when Sano and Jay didn't think I could ride that hoverboard. Sano would've made some kind of bet, pushing me to prove him wrong. But since he wasn't here, there was no one to bet with.

I set the bucket down and picked up one of the small red rings, turning it over in my hand. It was lighter than I expected. No wonder they bounced off the bottles so easily.

"Even when you're playing a game, you look so focused." Lacey's voice broke my concentration. I glanced up to see her watching me with amusement.

"Sorry," she giggled. "I just noticed you always look super focused in class when we're doing work. And just now, you had the same expression with the rings."

I blinked. "Really? I didn't know I had a 'look of concentration.'"

Now I felt oddly self-conscious. I had no idea she paid that much attention to me.

"It's not a bad thing," she reassured me. "That's probably why you always do so well. You'll get this too." She pointed to the bottles encouragingly.

I still had the ring in my hand. Taking aim, I picked a bottle and tossed it. It flew faster than I expected, landing awkwardly between the others.

"Is that really the best you can do?" Jay snickered at my failed attempt.

It really felt like old times—except this time, Lacey was here instead of Sano.

"Try again. You'll get it this time," Lacey said, handing me another ring.

Since the rings were so light, I knew I didn't need much force. This time, I flicked my wrist with just a little motion. The ring hit the neck of the bottle—but bounced off again.

"I knew I was right to get the bucket," Jay smirked. "Looks like you'll need them all."

"You almost had it that time. Just relax and try again. Third time's the charm, right?" Lacey encouraged, her voice full of confidence.

Meanwhile, Jay seemed more interested in betting against me. This game was more difficult than it looked. You'd think the bottles were moving with the way the rings kept bouncing off, but they stayed perfectly still.

I grabbed another ring and tossed it. Another near miss.

"You're super close. Just let it go—like this."

Lacey picked up a ring and flicked her wrist, letting it pop up a little higher than mine had. The ring spun in the air, landing around the neck of one of the bottles, teetered back and forth—and then settled neatly into place.

Her eyes widened. "No way! I got it? I've never won at this game before!"

She was shocked—and honestly, so was I. She landed one on her first try with barely any effort. The booth attendant handed her a small prize.

Jay whistled. "This is one for the record books. Kenny-Kens, looks like your title is about to be revoked. Lacey, how do you feel about being crowned the new champion?"

I shot him a look. "Hold on. I still have plenty of rings left. I'll get one of them."

Determined, I picked up another ring and tossed it. Then another. And another. But somehow, with every throw, I got worse.

I'd never struggled with something so simple before. Lacey had managed it with ease, so I knew it was possible. But for some reason, I just couldn't get it.

"At this rate, we're going to need another bucket," Jay teased. "Lacey, why don't you show him how it's done again?"

"That was a lucky shot. I doubt I could do it again," she admitted, picking up another ring and tossing it. It came close but bounced off.

"See?" She gave me a sheepish smile. "That first one was pure luck. I've played this game a bunch before, and that was the only time I've ever won. It's okay if you cant get it. It's your first try."

"Sorry, 'can't' isn't in my vocabulary. I'll get it," I assured her, gripping the next ring with renewed determination. Five left. That was plenty. I tossed one. It landed close—just like Lacey's had.

I replayed the way she threw hers in my head: the flick of her wrist, the slight lift as she let go. Mimicking her movements, I launched the next ring. It sailed through the air, dipped down, and—landed perfectly around the neck of a bottle.

"Hey, you got it! I knew you could do it!" Lacey jumped with excitement.

It had only taken me twenty tries to her one. But she was just as thrilled as if I'd gotten it on the first try.

"You still have three more. Why don't you go for a bigger prize?" Jay smirked, ever the instigator.

I glanced at the sign. Three rings landed meant a better prize. Might as well try. I threw the next one—miss. The next—landed right on the bottle in front of my first win.

"You're getting good at this! That's two in one game!" Lacey grinned.

I held up my last ring but hesitated. "Together, we got three. If you want, you can pick the bigger prize."

Her eyes widened. "Me? But you got two of them. You should choose."

"You landed one before I did. Besides—" I gestured toward the big stuffed animals lining the booth—"I think one of these suits you more than me."

I was never into stuffed bears and such. And if I really wanted one, I could just buy it.

"Really? Thanks, Ken!" She traded in her smaller prize, her dimples deepening as she hugged the new plush toy.

I smiled to myself. I'd wondered if today might feel awkward—hanging out one-on-one with a girl. But so far? It was going pretty well.

"I think I'm ready for another ride," I said, eager to keep the momentum going.

"I'm up for whatever you pick next." Lacey's smile lingered as she looked at me.

I turned to her, and for a second, our eyes locked. Something in my chest tightened as I held her gaze—just a small tug, unexpected but undeniable. I looked away, and so did she. What was that?

I didn't have time to figure it out. I needed to find another ride—fast. Scanning the fairgrounds, I searched for something, anything, to break the moment.

And that's when I saw it. Or rather—them.

"What do you—oh, my." Jay's voice dropped as he followed my gaze.

Striding toward us, Jenny waved wildly. "There you are!"

And right behind her—my dad and Jocelyn. Of all the places. Of all the people.

This cannot turn out well.

Chapter 13

"Good afternoon, little Kenneth. Jayson." Jocelyn greeted us with her usual polished tone.

"Good afternoon, Miss Baker. I see you all decided to enjoy this fine day at the fair as well?" Jay, ever the smooth talker, immediately switched into his most charming persona, flashing them a welcoming smile.

"I mentioned your little outing to Jenny, and she insisted on coming," my father explained. "We figured, why not see what all the excitement was about?" His gaze swept over me—then landed on Lacey.

We could pretend she wasn't with us, but that would only make him wonder why she kept following us around.

"Oh, Papa Masy, this is our little friend, Lacey. And Lacey, this is Kenny-Kens's father." Jay made the introduction sound effortless.

"Pleasure to meet you, Lacey," my father said, his expression unreadable. "Jayson, you didn't mention Ken had a friend joining you both."

Jay didn't even flinch. "We were just so eager to get here, it slipped my mind. Have you all had a chance to try anything yet? We were just about to head to another ride."

He handled it well, but I could tell—my dad wasn't letting this slide. Not yet.

Before anyone could say more, Jenny rushed forward and latched onto my arm, exactly like she always did.

"I want to go wherever Kenny is going!" she announced, practically beaming. "I didn't think I'd get to see you today. I'm so happy we ran into you!" She completely ignored Lacey.

I didn't even want to look at her. Not with Jenny clinging to me like this. And I couldn't pull away. Not with my father and Jocelyn standing right there. Unless Jenny moved on her own, Lacey was going to get the wrong idea.

"You sure are lucky to have spent the whole day with Kenny," Jenny finally acknowledged Lacey—but not in a way I liked. Then, tilting her head slightly, she added, "I hope you don't mind if I join you now."

I glanced at Lacey. The stuffed bear she'd won earlier was still in her arms, but her big, bright smile had dimmed. She was taking everything in—Jenny, my father, the sudden shift in atmosphere.

And then, with surprising ease, she smiled again.

"The more, the merrier," she said lightly. "We can all enjoy the fair together."

I blinked. I hadn't expected that. I figured she'd be scared off with everyone here. But Lacey didn't waver.

Instead, she looked straight at Jenny. And Jenny, still holding onto me, looked right back. This was not going to end well.

"Since Kenny-Kens picked the first ride, why don't you choose the next one?" Jay said to Lacey, his voice deliberately casual.

"I want to go on the Ferris wheel!" Jenny announced before Lacey could answer.

I sighed. "I was thinking of saving that for last." Lacey and I had already planned to make it our final ride. What had started as a fun outing was slowly turning into a family affair—and history proved that outings with my father never ended well.

"I don't mind going now," Lacey said.

123

She might be speaking up, but I could tell she was getting uncomfortable. Before, it had just been the two of us and Jay. Now, she was surrounded by people she didn't know.

"I've been on a Ferris wheel before. It's a nice little ride. I wouldn't mind going on it," Jocelyn added, her tone smooth, sealing my fate. Three against one. That was that.

We made our way over, Jenny clinging to one side of me while Lacey walked on the other. Jay trailed behind, and my father and Jocelyn led the way. It almost felt like I was being escorted—like a prisoner being marched to his next sentence. Before they showed up, I'd felt free. Now, it was as if I were back home, trapped under my father's watchful eye.

When we reached the Ferris wheel, my father and Jocelyn took a car together, leaving the rest of us to pile into another.

Just as I was about to sit down, Jenny clutched my arm.

"Kenny, can I sit next to you? I don't think I like heights that much."

I blinked. "Weren't you the one who wanted to get on this?"

"Yeah, but I didn't realize it was this high. I don't want to sit alone."

"There are four of us. It'll be two on each side. You wouldn't be sitting alone," I pointed out.

She pouted. "Jayson, is it okay if I sit with Kenny? I know you two are close, and you probably wanted to sit together."

Jay smirked like he was watching a movie play out in real time. "Oh, I didn't plan to sit with him. Jenny, dear, why not let Lacey sit with Kenny-Kens? I'm sure she'd prefer to sit with him over little ol' me. Plus, she's the guest today."

Jenny's gaze flicked to Lacey before landing on me. "Well, Kenny, who would you rather sit with?"

My stomach dropped. I did not see this coming. If I said I wanted to sit next to Lacey, it'd seem like I liked her. If I let Jenny sit next to me, she'd think I liked her.

Was this what Jay meant when he said getting involved with girls brought on a whole different world? Because I was starting to think he had a point.

"I just want to ride the Ferris wheel, so I don't mind where I sit," Lacey said, her voice light but unreadable. "I'll sit with you, Jay, since she really wants to sit with Ken."

She made the decision for everyone before I could even react. I exhaled, relieved—but now I wasn't sure if she'd gotten the wrong idea.

Jenny immediately slid into the seat next to me, settling in a little too comfortably. The ride began its slow ascent, creaking as it lifted us higher. None of us spoke at first. We just sat there, watching the fair shrink beneath us, the silence thick and awkward.

Then, Jenny shifted closer. "This is really high." She wrapped her arms around mine and leaned in. "Glad you're here to keep me calm. You're always helping me."

Usually, I wouldn't think twice about something like that, but with Lacey sitting across from us, her stuffed bear clutched in her lap, the words felt heavier. I knew I should say something, set a boundary—but I didn't know what or how.

Jay cleared his throat. "This sure is one way to start off your summer vacation. A nice day at the fair. I still can't believe you got Kenny-Kens so worked up over that ring toss, Lacey. He never gets that competitive."

Lacey's small smile was polite. "Well, we did get the big prize out of it. Thanks again for letting me have this." She hugged the bear slightly, like it was something to hold onto.

Jenny glanced at the prize before turning back to me. "Can you win me a prize too? We only ever hang out at your place. Since we're out, why not play a game for me?"

I tensed.

Jenny had always been a handful, but now, with Lacey here, she seemed impossible. She wasn't just ignoring her—she was staking a claim.

The rest of the day only got worse. Jenny never left my side, my father and Jocelyn hovered like watchdogs, and any freedom I'd had at the start of the day was gone. And just when I thought it was finally over, my dad insisted on coming with us to drop Lacey off so he could speak with her parents.

They seemed to like that he was involved. They didn't realize it just made everything more suffocating.

By the time we got home, Jocelyn and Jenny had left, and I retreated straight to my room. Jay was called into my dad's office.

What should have been a fun day had been completely wrecked. And now, Jay was probably going to get in trouble for the crime of letting me have a little freedom.

"Knock, knock." Jay's voice came from the doorway before he stepped inside. He didn't look happy. After a conversation with my father, I wouldn't expect him to.

"Let me guess, I'm on lockdown again?" I asked, already resigned.

"No, you're not on lockdown."

I blinked. "Wait—seriously?" That was unexpected. Usually, something bad followed a meeting in that office.

Jay sighed, rubbing the back of his neck. "You're not on lockdown per se... but if you want to go anywhere like that again, he has to take you."

I sat up straight. "What?"

"I did my best to get him to understand, trust me. That's why he's not outright forbidding you from going out. But until further notice, he wants to be wherever you go—just to make sure another 'incident' doesn't happen."

My jaw clenched. "You're joking. So, he won't even let you take me anywhere?"

"Unfortunately." Jay shrugged, looking genuinely apologetic. "I'm sorry, Kenny-Kens. I tried to reason with him, but it was either this or you spending your whole summer in his office. He wasn't exactly mad that Lacey was with us—he was mad that we didn't tell him. And, well... because she's a girl."

I let out a frustrated sigh. "Wasn't it punishment enough having Jenny stuck to me all day like glue? She wasn't even invited!"

Jay smirked. "You know, I was surprised. I didn't think she was the jealous type."

I frowned. "You think she was jealous?"

He gave me a look. "Do I think? Kenny-Kens, it was obvious. I mean, I know Jenny likes you, but she's never been that close. You two could've passed as conjoined twins the way she stuck to you today. And every time Lacey spoke? She had to jump in, making everything about you two. I didn't even want to say anything—I had no clue what she'd do if I did. Especially after that whole Ferris wheel fiasco."

I rubbed my face, groaning. "I figured she'd act different, but I didn't think it was because of jealousy."

Jay shook his head, laughing. "You've got a lot to learn, Kenny-Kens. Like I told you—women are a whole different world. You have to learn how to read them and how to understand them if you ever want to know what's really going on. And even then..." He shrugged. "Only a few can ever say they've cracked that code."

"At this rate, I don't think I'll be one of them." I sighed, leaning back against the bed. "Did you see how Lacey started acting? She barely said a word after the family showed up. She probably won't want to hang out again after being swarmed like that."

Jay shrugged. "You never know unless you ask."

I shook my head. "Even if I did, I don't want to bring her around with my dad babysitting. He's busy in the summer so he can take time off for the villa trip. He might as well have just put me on lockdown—because that's what this is."

Jay sighed. "I'm sorry, Kenny-Kens. I really did try to change his mind."

"Wouldn't have mattered. Nothing ever does." I exhaled, staring at the ceiling. "Sorry you got blamed for it. I didn't exactly tell him the plan either. Just... times like this, I really wish Mom was still with him. She could've at least tried to change his mind."

Jay was quiet for a moment before saying, "Well, that's one place he can't stop you from going—seeing her. And he'll let you go with me. Maybe that can be our next adventure."

I looked over at him.

"You haven't visited since school let out," he added. "She'd be happy to see you."

"That's true..." My voice trailed off.

Jay frowned. "What? You don't want to see her?"

"No, that's not it." I hesitated, staring at my hands. "I was just thinking about earlier. That ring toss game reminded me how much I miss having Sano around. And now that it's summer... it's just weird. We'd all be betting on who was going to lose during the volleyball games at the villa. It's not going to be the same without him. Or Mom." I exhaled. "It's just been on my mind today. You know, when Jenny wasn't squeezing my arm to death."

Jay huffed a laugh. "Hearing that just makes me think going to see your mom is an even better idea. Starting summer like this—especially with Papa Masy holding you down—is going to be rough. At least seeing her might help you feel a little more at ease."

"Yeah, I suppose you're right. But we'll probably have to wait a while." I sighed. "Sounds like my father isn't too trusting right now. I don't want to risk losing my chances to see her too."

I knew he wouldn't stop me from visiting my mom. I just didn't want to ask him for anything right now. A part of me was convinced he'd planned to come to the fair all along—just to check up on me. And that wasn't something he would've thought up on his own. If he really wanted to keep tabs on me, he'd either ask outright or send someone else to do it.

But lately, he was different. Ever since he started seeing Jocelyn.

I never would've expected him to show up at a place like that. It's not like he enjoys fairs, crowds, or spending extra time with me. So what else is he willing to do now?

Chapter 14

"I was beginning to worry you didn't want to see me anymore," Mom pouted, heading into the kitchen.

"It's been a little rough for the little man lately," Jay said, casually dropping into a chair at the dining table.

Mom immediately turned back. "Really? Something going on I need to know about?"

"Oh, nothing serious. Just Kenny-Kens growing up into a little man."

"Jay…" I shot him a look. We hadn't even been here ten minutes, and he was already running his mouth.

"Oh, don't be embarrassed now," he teased, grinning.

Mom folded her arms. "A man, you say? Jayson, what have you been getting my son into?" She walked into the dining room, eyeing him suspiciously.

Jay leaned back in his chair, all smug. "Don't go blaming me. It's the bloodline, I tell you! You know we're irresistible."

Mom raised a brow. "Ken, do you want to tell me what Jayson's going on about before I have to punish both of you?"

"It's nothing, really," I muttered. "Last week, we just went to the fair with someone from my class." I kept it vague, but I knew it wouldn't be enough.

Mom smirked. "I see… And what's her name?"

I sighed, knowing there was no way around this. "Lacey."

Mom's smile grew. "Lacey is a nice name. I'm sure she's just as nice. But tell me—whose idea was it to go to the fair? I know it wasn't yours." She turned straight to Jay, who immediately sat up, bracing for interrogation.

"So here's what happened," he began, all dramatic. "We're at the bakery, just minding our own business, enjoying some dessert, when this cute-as-a-button girl walks in and starts chatting up Kenny-Kens. It's been so boring lately, I figured we should start the summer off with a little fun at the fair." He shrugged like it was the most innocent thing in the world.

I sighed. If this was the story he told my father, no wonder the man wasn't happy. Now to see how Mom took it.

She tilted her head. "I'm all for you having fun. But she better stay a girl 'friend'—not a girlfriend." She made sure to emphasize the difference.

"I know you're growing up and got all my looks, but no dating at this age. My parents always told me to wait until I was sixteen. I might have been fifteen when I had my first boyfriend, but let's keep it at that." She gave me a pointed look before shifting her gaze to Jay. "Weren't you, like, fifteen—or maybe even fourteen—when Jamie started asking me what to do with you?"

Jay let out a laugh. "Fourteen, and that one is complicated," he said, rubbing the back of his neck. "There were three girls who all thought I was dating them, and I had no idea. I mean, I did like one of them, but once that mess started, I backed away from all of them."

Mom shot him a look, unimpressed. "See, Ken, don't go being like this one over here. As a woman, I'll tell you—it's not easy dealing with us. Especially when you play with our emotions." She stared daggers at Jay, who just shrugged like it was no big deal.

"I'm happy you've found a little friend to talk to and hang out with," she continued, turning her attention back to me. "Just keep it that way for a couple more years. I'm not ready to have *the talk*—not this soon."

Mom wasn't angry, and she wasn't upset. She was just… happy that I had a friend. My father, on the other hand, went straight to interrogating Lacey's family the moment he met her. Mom just told me not to date and was fine with us spending time together. There was always a difference in how my parents saw things, but seeing it play out like this made it even more obvious. It reminded me exactly why I wanted her around when all of this started. She definitely would've kept me out of trouble.

"Aside from making me feel old knowing my son is growing up, how's everything else?" she asked, shaking her head with a smile. "Have you talked to Sano lately?"

She always asked about Sano. Every time I visited, she wanted to know how he was doing. She knew we'd had limited contact for a while, and when he finally started talking to me again, she was relieved.

"I haven't heard from him since last week," I admitted.

Her expression shifted. "Really? Did something happen?"

"Nothing happened, I don't think. He just hasn't responded to me."

Jay frowned. "That doesn't have anything to do with what I asked you to do, does it?"

Mom's gaze snapped to him. "What did you ask him to do?"

Jay held up his hands. "I just wanted him to ask about Sano's summer plans. Maybe see if he was thinking about visiting."

I sighed. "I didn't ask him."

Jay narrowed his eyes. "Why not?"

I hesitated before answering. "I was afraid he wouldn't want to talk about coming back here."

Mom nodded, understanding. "I think that was smart. He already waited so long just to reach out to you again. Make sure he's comfortable first before diving into that. Maybe send him another message, just to check in."

I considered it. She was probably right. After a pause, I looked at her. "Did you know anything about his mother?"

Her expression softened. Out of everyone, she was the one person I felt comfortable bringing this up with.

"I knew her for a short time before I realized who she was."

"What do you mean by that?"

"Before I moved out here with your dad, I lived near her and used to see her at a store I frequented. We got acquainted after I helped her find a job—she'd been searching for one. But that was around the same time I moved in with your father, so I didn't see much of her after that." She paused, as if lost in thought. "She was super sweet—a very kind woman. But she was sick a lot."

"Sick?" I echoed.

"I probably shouldn't be telling you this, but she had some health issues. She didn't like to talk about them. It was personal. But that's also why I agreed to take in Sano."

"But if she wanted to keep him, why did she give him up?" I asked. She didn't answer right away. Her eyes narrowed in thought.

"I'm sorry, sweetie. I'd rather not explain that. After a long court case and months of uncertainty, we all agreed not to talk about it anymore—to keep Sano safe."

"What could happen to him? He was just a baby, right? It's not like he did anything."

"It wasn't him that was the issue. As sweet as she was, she was determined—and she had a very good lawyer. Your father was almost deemed unfit to care for him."

"Unfit?" I frowned. "Wouldn't most people consider living in a mansion a pretty good life?"

"He didn't have the mansion yet. The house we lived in was still very nice, but that wasn't the only thing they considered," she explained. It was clear she didn't want to talk about it. Jay was sitting on the edge of his seat, hanging on every word.

"It got to the point where they even considered taking you away, too." She placed a hand on my shoulder.

"Me?"

"It was a bad, scary time. You were still less than a year old. I quit my job and stayed with you around the clock, terrified I'd wake up one day and you'd be gone. So, believe me when I say it's not something I like to think about."

"I didn't mean to upset you," I said, feeling guilty. Now I understood why no one wanted to talk about this. A lot had happened back then. I decided not to push her for more answers. "I'll message Sano again and let you know if he's okay."

"Only if you really want to." She rubbed my shoulder.

"I always want to know what he's up to, so it's no problem." I reached into my pocket, pulled out my phone, and sent him a message. I had been hesitant at first when my father asked, but seeing my mom like this—actually asking about him—made me want to do it.

"While you're doing that, why don't we get something started for lunch?" Jay stood and headed for the kitchen.

"If you think I'm letting you cook in my kitchen without me, you are sadly mistaken," Mom said, following him.

"Oh, I didn't expect to." Jay handed her a skillet. "You can help too when you're done," he called to me.

I was already done and joined them in the kitchen. I had no idea what was on the menu, and I didn't think they did either. Jay must've sensed the tension and wanted to shift the mood. Moving around the small space, bumping into each other, made any lingering heaviness fade away.

Mom didn't have many options, so we ended up making burgers and homemade fries. We were just about finished when I checked my phone and saw a message from Sano. But something about his reply felt off.

— *Do you really care if I'm okay?*

I didn't understand why he would say that. I had been careful not to upset him. I was still thinking about how to respond when another message came in.

— *You don't need to keep worrying about me. I'm fine here. You seem to be fine without me too.*

"Something wrong, Kenny-Kens?" Jay noticed the confusion on my face. I showed him the messages.

"Was it something I said?" I asked.

"I don't think so. It doesn't look like you said anything that would make him react like this." Jay scrolled through my previous messages.

"What do you think happened?"

"Hard to tell. We don't know what's going on over there, but there has to be a reason he said that."

"Something wrong?" Mom called from the kitchen. She had already been worried once—I didn't want her worrying again.

"No." Jay and I said it at the same time.

"Okay, now I'm suspicious."

"Nothing to worry about in here," Jay said smoothly. "He was just a little confused about something, but it's all good."

"I better not find out you're giving him 'Jay' advice with this Lacey girl, or else I'll give you a 'Kelly' talk. And you know mine involves more actions than words."

"Now, now, Auntie. It's nothing like that. Save that power for the real opponents. You know you can't ruin this look." Jay followed her back into the kitchen.

"You might be taller and younger, but don't think I won't take you on."

"That's exactly what I'm worried about—because I know you will." They both laughed.

We had successfully dodged another heavy conversation. Leave it to Jay to always take a hit for me.

Still, I couldn't shake the feeling that something was wrong. Why was Sano still talking like this after all these months? It was one thing when he acted this way while he was here, but he's been gone for so long now. What was going on?

I started to feel like I was walking on eggshells, constantly second-guessing what I said or did around him. But that hadn't helped before— he still left without any of us knowing. We were all devastated by what happened, but that didn't mean I could just let him act however he wanted.

So, I told him exactly how I felt about his attitude. He might not be able to forgive everyone for what happened, but that didn't mean I forgave him for leaving.

I tried not to let it bother me. I tried not to let his "*I really did make the right choice*" reply ruin my time with my mom. I put my phone away, determined to enjoy the rest of the day with her before I had to return to my prison cell.

"I still can't believe you're going to the eighth grade in the fall. Where has the time gone?" We all sat at the table after dinner with a bowl of ice cream.

"Soon, you'll be in high school, then college, and then you'll be all grown up." Her voice carried a quiet sadness.

"As I'm always reminded, I'm still young, so it'll be a while before that happens." I tried to reassure her.

"I know. Just thinking about how fast time has gone already."

"Don't worry, Kenny-Kens. She did the same with me, and I'm not even her child. Brace yourself," Jay teased.

"Since you aren't my child, let me have this moment with mine," Mom pouted.

"It's okay, Mom. I know it'll be hard. So let's just enjoy the time we have while I'm still young."

"See, only a growing and mature young man would say that. My baby is leaving me!" Mom dramatically placed her hands over her face, pretending to cry.

"Do I need to bring out the tissue?" Jay teased.

"No need." She sniffed. "This paper towel will work just fine." She dabbed at the corners of her eyes. She had actually teared up a little.

"I tell you this every time you visit, and I'm not planning to stop. Whenever you need me or anything at all, just let me know. I know living with your dad isn't always easy, so don't hesitate to come to me when you need a break, okay?"

She knew he was strict and liked to keep me cooped up in the house. Though I hadn't told her that things had only gotten worse since she left, I still felt relief every time she reassured me. Sometimes, I wanted to ask if I could just stay here. But after hearing about the custody battle they'd gone through over Sano, I couldn't risk putting them through another fight over me. And I didn't want to worry her by saying anything.

By the time Jay and I got back home, it was evening. We were expected to return before dark, so we had to leave early. Once we got home, I finally decided to reply to Sano. I still didn't understand why he had gotten so upset, but I couldn't keep pretending it didn't bother me. I waited for his response, but it never came...

Days went by and weeks came through, and that's when I realized—I wasn't going to get a reply. My father found out that they were moving, but they hadn't given him their new address. Sano's number changed, and he never bothered to give me the new one. If I had known that the shadow I'd seen that night would be the last time I'd ever see him, I would've at least told him to be safe...

I never thought anything could feel worse than knowing my own brother had left me without a second thought. That was until I heard the news—news I never expected.

There was only one week left before school started. We were spending our final day at our villa home by the lake, enjoying the last moments of our week-long stay before heading back home. Jay, my father, and I were there, along with—unsurprisingly—Jocelyn. We all sat around the fire pit, waiting for the BBQ to finish cooking, when my father stood up to make an announcement.

"I hope we've all had another wonderful time resting and relaxing here this year. It was our first vacation with this wonderful woman," Dad said, gesturing to Jocelyn.

"I'm truly grateful to have been able to join you all at this beautiful home. I hope you'll allow me to return again," Jocelyn said, her voice warm and sincere.

"With that being said," Dad began, his tone more serious now, "Jocelyn, I formally invite you here—and everywhere else I go—for as long as you'll have me." He turned to face her, his eyes filled with a depth I hadn't seen before.

"I stand before my family today to ask you—will you be my wife and join us in all our future events and adventures?"

A waiter approached, carrying a covered plate. He lifted the lid, revealing an open box with a diamond ring inside

"Kenneth... I'm speechless. Are you serious?" Jocelyn pressed a hand to her chest, her eyes wide as they darted between my father and the ring. She was stunned. Jay was stunned. And so was I. But our shock felt completely different from hers.

"When have you ever known me to joke about something like this?" My father laughed. "I would never say something so important in front of the people who mean the most to me if I didn't mean it. I've thought about this for a long time. I only hope you feel the same and will accept my proposal."

His words were steady, sincere. He was completely serious. I had no idea what to say. This wasn't something I'd expected—especially not here, not now. My gaze flickered to Jay, who met my eyes. For once, there was no quip, no smooth retort. He looked just as lost for words as I felt. It was one of those rare moments when I saw Jay unsure of how to react, and that unsettled me more than anything else.

"Yes, I will. I'll marry you, Kenneth," Jocelyn said, a tear slipping down her cheek.

The servants clapped and whistled in celebration. From across the lake, the sound of fireworks shattered the stillness. The sky lit up in a thousand colors, and music began to play. One of the servants popped open a bottle of champagne. It was supposed to be a joyous occasion.

But I couldn't shake the feeling that this wasn't the celebration it seemed.

I wanted nothing more than for it to be a nightmare I could wake up from.

"This marks the end of a wonderful summer," my father said, his voice brimming with pride. "Ken, Jayson, I hope you'll stand by my side and take part in the wedding."

"Well, first, congratulations! This was unexpected, but I'm so glad it turned out well. I'll help however I can, Papa Masy," Jay chimed in.

I'd been around Jay long enough to recognize when he slipped into character, following the script he'd been handed. It wasn't a surprise—Jay was always good at playing his part. But in that moment, all I could think was how badly I wanted to rip that script to shreds and toss it into the lake. Nothing about this made sense.

He never told us he wanted to marry her. It hadn't even been that long since he divorced Mom, and now he expected Jay and me to be in this wedding? My stomach twisted, a heavy knot forming in my chest. I couldn't sit there a second longer—I had to get out.

I left without a word, walking away from the table and heading for anywhere but there. I had just started coming to terms with everything. Trying to move on. Trying to accept all that had happened this year. But this? This, I couldn't accept. Marrying someone else? I barely even knew this woman, and now he wanted me to call her my new mom?

"Kenny-Kens."

I didn't need to turn around to know it was Jay. He had found me standing by the lake, the fireworks reflecting off the water in brilliant colors.

"If you're here to talk me into accepting this, don't bother," I said, not bothering to mask the bitterness in my voice.

"Please, Kenny-Kens, don't assume that's why I'm here," he sighed, his voice softer than usual.

I turned to face him. His expression was troubled—worn down by something I couldn't quite place. It wasn't a look I'd ever seen on him before.

"I was glad you walked away," he admitted quietly. "Between the two of us, it would've been bad if I had."

"What are we supposed to do about this?" I asked, my voice thick with frustration. "How can we just... accept this?"

"Not much we can do," Jay said, shaking his head. "He never once asked either of us about this decision. It's obvious that whatever we say, it won't change his mind. I've stood by Papa Masy through a lot, but honestly? I don't know if I can stand by this."

Hearing Jay say that was like a punch to the gut. He had never gone against my father. To hear him doubt Dad now? That was a first.

"I knew she was coming around more and more, but I never thought he'd actually ask her to marry him," I started, staring out to the water. "We've never really talked. She's never made an effort to have a real conversation with me—just 'hi,' 'bye,' and 'Jenny is here today.'"

"It's frustrating, I know," Jay said, his voice low. "And I can't even tell you to stop thinking about it. We could try talking to Papa Masy about it, but let's be real—our opinions won't change his mind."

The vacation to the villa had already been awkward with her here. This just sealed the deal—an unwanted visit turned into an uncomfortable spectacle.

My father had refused to cancel the trip this year, even after everything that happened at the beginning of the year. I had hoped that this last day would pass quickly. But instead, time seemed to stretch on endlessly, each second dragging longer than the last. His proposal replayed in my head like a broken record, every word echoing louder and louder, until it drowned out everything else.

I avoided him for the rest of the night. After Jay and I had tried to make sense of this new development, I retreated to my room, wanting nothing more than to be left alone.

Night came and went in a blur, and morning crept up before I was ready. We were all getting ready to head back home when I heard a knock at my door. I assumed it was Jay, but when I opened it, I saw Jocelyn standing there instead.

"I hope you don't mind me stopping by. I know you're packing, but I just wanted to see you before we left," she said, her smile too bright, her presence too sudden.

"I'm done packing," I replied, keeping my tone neutral. The thought of going home had kept me up for hours, eager to just finish this trip and put it behind me.

"That's good then." She stepped further into my room, her eyes scanning the space as if assessing it. "Listen, about yesterday..." She hesitated, like she was carefully choosing her words. "I was really happy when your father proposed to me, but I have to admit, I was a little sad when you took off like that. I don't want things to be awkward between us. I hope, in the coming days, we can get along. I would hate for it to feel uncomfortable just because you might not be ready to accept that your dad has already moved on."

She smiled at me, but the smile felt forced, like she was trying too hard to be pleasant. There was something off about it, a strange undercurrent that made the air feel colder.

"It might take you some time to adjust, and I understand that," she continued. "But let's try to make this work since I'll be around a lot more from now on—whether you're happy about it or not. Your father is, and that's what matters most."

And with that, she turned and walked out, her heels clicking sharply against the floor as she left. A chill ran through me. I couldn't pinpoint exactly what it was—her tone, her words, or the way her smile lingered like something rehearsed—but there was something unsettling about the whole conversation.

Suddenly, I felt it—the change. A shift that I hadn't seen coming.

Whether it was my father who was changing, or if it was me, I wasn't sure. But something was different. Things were about to change.

I grabbed my bag and made my way downstairs. What used to be a relaxing trip to the villa was now over. The carefree days of summer had slipped through my fingers, leaving nothing but a tense, heavy air. The new school year loomed ahead, its arrival as unavoidable as the changes that had been creeping into my life. And for once, I welcomed the distraction.

Though deep down, something told me I was going to need more than a school year to sort through everything that had already happened—and whatever else was yet to come.

Chapter 15

Time and time again, I find myself sitting in this office, across from the world-renowned businessman. Surprisingly, it's not always because I'm in trouble. This time, my father has something else he wants to "discuss" with me. Most people find him intimidating, but after sixteen years of this, I've learned there's no reason to be overly anxious.

"I don't understand what was so bad about Ashley," he says, diving right in. I figure this is about me breaking up with his latest "perfect match."

"You said she was 'a bit ambitious,'" I begin, "but you conveniently left out the part about her being a bit acquisitive as well," I sigh.

"She seemed like a respectable and suitable young girl."

"Every day, she asked me to buy her a new car so she could travel the country over break. I don't know where you're finding these people, but could we stop this game already? If you keep this up, we'll be bankrupt in no time."

Ever since he found out I dated Lacey during my freshman year, it's been his mission to find me someone he deems "fitting."

"Ken, you're sixteen now, and I'm trying to meet you halfway. I understand you want to make your own choices, but at your age, I just want to make sure you aren't making mistakes."

"Shouldn't I be the one to decide if I've made a mistake or not? You dictating my choices won't change anything. There was nothing wrong with Lacey. You broke us up just because you went to her house

143

once and thought it was '*a little below average,*'" I say, emphasizing his claim.

"Jenny also thought she wasn't good for you," he adds.

"Jenny doesn't think anyone other than herself is good for me," I snap.

"I still don't understand why you refuse her. She's been nothing but a delight and does just about everything for you."

I exhale sharply, irritation rising. "Don't you have some papers to sign or something? I don't want to talk about this anymore."

He knows I've never been interested in Jenny, yet he always finds a way to slip her into the conversation when he gets the chance.

"Alright. We'll discuss this at a later time—hopefully, one where we can come to a compromise," he says, his tone clipped and edged with annoyance. I don't bother responding. I simply get up and walk out.

My dating life has become some kind of business deal my father's trying to broker. He should focus on his own relationship with that woman instead of obsessing over mine.

"Don't you seem thrilled," Jennifer says, her voice dripping with sarcasm as I'm about to head upstairs. "I take it he didn't handle your breakup news too well?"

"If you're asking whether or not I'm considering Jenny now, the answer is still no," I reply, continuing toward my room. I don't have much against Jennifer. I just don't want to see either of them right now.

Jenny's always been nice to me. But I've never been able to see her as anything other than someone permanently attached to my side. Now that she and her sister live here, her affection has only gotten more intense. I was suffocating before. Now? I feel like I'm drowning…

"Kenny, can I come in?" It's Jenny, of course, knocking at my door. I'm already lying in bed, so I mutter, "Come in."

"Why are you so down? Did you have a bad day?" she asks, stepping inside and sitting on the edge of my bed as if she has every right to be there.

I sigh, the weight of everything pressing on me. "Do you want something? Because I'd really like to be alone right now."

"You know, I'm glad you dumped that Amy girl."

"Her name was Ashley," I correct her, not in the mood for her casual tone.

"Well, it doesn't matter anymore since she's out of the picture," she shrugs. "I could tell from the beginning she didn't really care about you. So, if you need to talk to someone, you can always talk to me. Seeing you so down always brings me down too."

The words are soft, like she's trying to be sweet, but I've heard them a thousand times. No matter if I'm fighting with my dad or just exhausted, she always pulls the same line. But then, I feel her hand caress the side of my leg. That? That's new.

"What are you doing?" I ask, my voice tight, my body stiffening.

"When we were younger, you used to let me hold your arm or get close to you," she says, voice low and almost pleading.

I exhale sharply, sitting up quickly, moving farther away from her. "Jenny, times have changed. But what hasn't changed is how I feel about you. I'm sorry, but I'm just not interested."

The words come out sharper than I'd intended, but I have to be blunt with her. She never takes a hint. She doesn't say anything. She just gets up and runs out of my room, the door slamming softly behind her. I'm definitely going to hear about this from Jennifer later. I roll my eyes. Fine. I'll take it—just as long as I get a moment alone.

"Did you really have to send her off crying like that?" Jay's voice comes through the door.

I can't help but laugh bitterly. "You know, I'm really starting to miss the days when I felt like I was the only one in this house." I sigh again.

Jay opens the door and steps inside, shutting it behind him. "I take it your talk with Papa Masy didn't go too well?"

"Did you think it would?" I asked, my voice flat.

Jay smirked. "What's the plan now?"

"Finish out these last few weeks as a sophomore. Then the rest of high school, college. And after that? Spend my life as a rich loner."

"Don't forget good-looking, too." He grinned, trying to lighten the mood.

I rolled my eyes. "I get A's in all my classes, finish all my schoolwork, and do just about everything I'm told. And yet, it still feels like I'm doing something wrong."

Jay leaned back, looking more serious. "Have you talked to Lacey since the breakup?"

I scoffed. "Thanks to Jennifer and Jenny, she doesn't even look in my direction anymore. It's probably a blessing Jenny insisted on private school. It would've been so much worse if she was here to keep '*handling things.*'" I air-quoted the last part for emphasis. Since Jennifer and I go to the same school, it's like she's Jenny's personal spy, keeping tabs on everything she doesn't like.

"I didn't think it would get this bad," Jay admitted. "But after Papa Masy got married and those two moved in, It's like everything's changed around here."

"I still don't get why we're taking care of them," I muttered, the frustration creeping back. I found out their parents had passed away in an accident a couple of years ago. But how they ended up here—living with us when we're not even blood-related—was something I couldn't wrap my head around.

"If I had an answer, I'd give it to you, but I'm still not sure myself. I let it slide since it was under... unfortunate circumstances. But it was supposed to be temporary." He met my gaze, his expression serious. "It's been well over a year now."

I nodded. Jay had put up with them just like I had, but even he was starting to crack under the weight of it all.

"Have you seen my mom recently?" I asked, shifting the conversation to something else.

"I actually just left her place. She's getting ready to go out of town with Isiah tomorrow," Jay said.

"So, they hit it off that well?" I asked, trying to process the fact that my mom was dating again. It felt strange. But if my father could remarry so quickly, I figured I could accept that she deserved to find her own happiness, too.

"She seems to like him a lot. She said if she can survive this trip with him, then he's a keeper. If not, she'll let him down gently."

"I doubt the 'gently' part." I tried to laugh, but it came out more like a sigh. Even my mom had better luck with relationships than I did.

It wasn't helping that I didn't trust many people these days. More and more, people were recognizing me as part of the Masidone fortune, and I'd had enough of people using me for my name. Even friendships felt transactional—too many hidden motives. If I ever wanted something that felt real, I'd have to leave. Move somewhere new. Somewhere no one knew my name.

That's when it hit me.

"Hey, Jay," I started, "remember that girl you had investigated?"

"Oh no, not this again." Jay groaned, rubbing his temples like he was dealing with a headache.

"Hey, I haven't brought this up in years."

"And I was hoping it stayed in the past."

"You think her parents ever got in the company?"

Jay shot me a look, clearly not thrilled with where this was going. "Have you seen her around school?"

"No, but I haven't exactly been looking," I admitted.

Jay hated the idea of me getting involved with someone who wasn't part of our world. But she didn't live out here. She didn't know me. She couldn't judge me like everyone else. By now, she'd probably forgotten the whole incident.

"Well..." Jay hesitated, the shift in his tone making me sit up a little straighter.

I narrowed my eyes. "Well, what? You know something?"

He hesitated before speaking again. "Remember that time Papa Masy needed me to rush some papers to him at the company? While I was there, he was talking to this woman—fine as wine—and he referred to her as Mrs. Macky. If memory serves me right, that was the last name of that girl. But it could also be a coincidence."

"Why didn't you tell me that?" I asked, frustration edging my voice.

"I thought you'd moved on, so I figured it didn't matter. It's been years. I was hoping it wasn't something you were still thinking about."

"It wasn't, really. But since nothing's working out here, I figured I'd try something new. Explore some new territory." I shrugged, feeling the weight of my own words.

"And now what? If she's not at your school, she could still be living in that other city. You can't just go out there."

"Maybe I can," I protested, folding my arms defiantly.

"Kenny-Kens..." Jay's tone was cautious, but I could see his skepticism.

"Come on, Jay. Haven't I suffered enough? Don't you think it's time for some fun around here? Don't you miss the days of sneaking out and 'forgetting' to mention the important details to my father about what we were up to?" I grinned, feeling the stirrings of rebellion.

"I don't miss the trouble…" he muttered, but I could hear the faintest hint of nostalgia.

"Who said there's going to be trouble? Who taught me everything I know?" I shot him a knowing look.

"Yours truly," he sang, rolling his eyes.

"And do you really doubt your own guidance?" I raised an eyebrow.

Jay sighed, clearly giving in. "What exactly have you already planned to do?"

"A little research," I said, getting off the bed and heading for my father's office. He had plans with Jocelyn, so now was my chance.

I stepped into his newly remodeled office, the smell of fresh wood and polished leather filling the air. Despite the upgrades, he was still old-fashioned enough to keep hard copies of everything in case anything ever happened.

I moved to his desk and started searching the drawers. One of the first folders I pulled out was exactly what I was looking for. I flipped through the pages, skimming for the name "Macky," until I found it about halfway through. Now I just needed to confirm that this was her mother and not someone else.

"Anything I can help you search for, son?"

I froze, my heart skipping a beat as I looked up to see my father stepping into the room. Either his plans with Jocelyn had been canceled, or he'd set up some kind of alarm in here. Either way, I wasn't prepared.

"Not exactly. I found what I was looking for," I said, forcing a tight, awkward smile. My mind raced, scrambling for an explanation. If I didn't come up with something convincing, I could kiss my chances of getting out of this room intact goodbye.

"And that would be?" His voice was sharp, his eyes narrowing in suspicion.

"I heard that the parents of someone I know work at your company, and I wanted to see for myself. Now that I've found out, I figured I'd make it easier for you to find them."

"And why exactly would I need to find them?" His arms folded across his chest, and I could tell he wasn't buying my story. I might have acted too quickly on this. If I ever want to see the light of day again, I'll have to tell him everything.

I shifted uncomfortably, knowing I was in too deep now. "Because—I'm interested in their daughter. Thought I'd have you check them out, see if they're to your liking."

"This is quite a shift from just a moment ago when you stormed out of here in a fury."

I shrugged, trying to play it cool. "What can I say? I'm a teenager with emotions." My attempt at humor fell flat.

"That much is true," he said, his gaze still skeptical. "However, you don't usually change your mind so easily. Forgive me for feeling a bit dubious about your story."

I swallowed hard. I was running out of options. "Would I have a reason to lie? Look, the person I was confirming is right here." I handed him the file, my hands shaking slightly.

He took it, glancing at the contents without saying a word. When he saw the name, his brows furrowed.

"Mrs. Macky, is it? She's one of the promising workers I've had my eye on since she joined a year ago. Not from around here... How exactly do you know she has a daughter?"

"We've met, obviously." I kept it vague, hoping the answer would satisfy him. He didn't press further, which was a small victory. I wasn't about to risk elaborating—especially since he doesn't know she was a part of the red-faced and bruised incident.

"So, are you asking me to speak with Mrs. Macky about setting something up between you and her daughter?" His tone was sharp—like he was dissecting my every word.

I straightened up, trying to appear confident. "Judging by the names on your desk, you're still playing this matchmaking game for me. We both know how well that's worked out." I let the bitterness slip through, but only a little. "So, maybe one last try—my pick. You said yourself you already have an interest in her mother."

I hadn't planned on taking this risk until I'd done my own digging at school. But after the break-in at his work office, he no longer trusted anyone in his private space—not even me—without a solid reason. And I wasn't as quick on my feet as Jay to come up with anything more plausible.

"And if I don't approve?" he asked, raising an eyebrow.

I shrugged, feigning indifference. "Why not save that discussion for after you've spoken with her?"

"Ken, I know you've been dealing with a lot lately. But the chances of this happening are slim to none. So, I think it's best you forget about it and go back to your room—before I reopen the one next door, since you seem so eager to be near me again." He motioned to the room next to his office, the infamous "punishment room."

I froze. The room, once a place where Sano and I were confined for missteps, now served as a holding cell for confiscated phones and computers. He hadn't threatened me with it in a while, but the idea of spending more time there was unappealing to say the least.

"You know," I began, my voice low, trying to push through the discomfort, "it's been a long time since I've actually felt any real fun or excitement. Last time was probably with Lacey. But, because a certain someone assumed the one person I actually liked was bad for me, I haven't gotten the chance to enjoy anything else."

I let the words hang in the air, hoping they'd land with some impact. "You always say you want what's best for me, but I have yet to see it."

We fight all the time, but this was the first time I'd ever said something like this outright. I must really be going crazy from being stuck in this house.

"We'll discuss this another time," my father said, his tone final. "I only came back to grab something I mistakenly left behind. I'll conveniently misplace the memory of finding you in my office this time. So, I hope you don't try anything like this again for me to remember it happened twice."

The weight of his words settled between us—a quiet threat, veiled in civility. It wasn't just a statement; it was a warning. His workstations were sacred ground. I quickly returned the folder to its rightful place, shutting the drawer with more care than I would've liked to admit. We both walked out in silence, and I headed back to my room. Walking away unscathed felt like some twisted form of luck, but I knew it was only temporary.

When I opened the door, Jay was sprawled across my bed, his eyes trained on the ceiling as if contemplating the meaning of life itself. "Should I call a doctor now? I need to make sure everything's okay in that head of yours."

I dropped into my chair with a sigh, running a hand through my hair. "Go ahead. At least that way, I'll be out of here for a few days."

Jay smirked but didn't push the issue. The truth was, lately, it was always something—my father getting on my case, humoring the girls he arranges for me, or Jenny constantly vying for my attention. The peace I once had was gone…

My time studying had become just another distraction, another place to hide from the chaos that had become my life. I buried myself in textbooks, not because I wanted to but because it was the one place where I could pretend that everything wasn't falling apart.

Summer arrived, but it was no escape. The warmth of the season only seemed to intensify the pressure. I occasionally got out—or more accurately forced out somewhere with Jenny and Jennifer. I went along with it, mostly because I couldn't stand staring at my walls any longer. Jenny thought I was coming around, that I'd change my mind, but I never did. My feelings for her were nonexistent. She was a distraction, nothing more.

And so, I settled into a routine. A predictable, suffocating routine that was clearly not going to break anytime soon. My father had insisted I learn the ropes of his company, study his every move. With junior year almost behind me, senior year on the horizon, he figured it was time I had a solid foundation in management. As if any of it mattered. I wasn't looking for a life in business; I was just trying to survive it.

"I want to congratulate you on taking more of an interest in the business," my father said, his eyes scanning the documents I'd handed him. He didn't even look up as he spoke, but I could hear the approval in his voice. It felt like an odd compliment.

With a pause, he set the papers aside, his expression becoming more thoughtful. "With that said, I thought I'd bring up something you may or may not still be interested in."

"What's that?" I asked cautiously. I had a feeling this wasn't going to be something I could easily dismiss. Anything he found 'interesting' usually meant more of his own agenda being thrust onto me.

"After significant research, evaluations, and a considerable amount of thought, I've finally arranged something with Mrs. Macky."

I blinked, leaning forward. "You mean this whole time you've actually been considering it?"

"I had to make sure she was worth the time. She's an outstanding employee, and she was thrilled at the idea of arranging something between you and her daughter," he explained, his voice casual, as if this was all just part of the plan.

I couldn't believe it. Months ago, I'd brought this up half-jokingly, figuring it would be forgotten or brushed off. I hadn't expected him to actually follow through.

"I only have one reservation," he added, glancing at me with an unreadable expression.

"What's that?" I asked, my gut tightening.

"She and her husband have a temporary home here. Their daughter didn't want to transfer schools, so she stays with a friend's family most of the time. But if this arrangement were to move forward, they'd relocate for the time being, and that would mean you'd go stay with them." He let the words hang in the air, as if testing me, waiting for my reaction.

"Stay... as in live with them?" I repeated, my voice slow, as if trying to process the absurdity of it. I couldn't believe what I was hearing.

"Yes." He nodded, his eyes narrowing slightly. "Mrs. Macky has quite the imagination. I can see you're just as against this idea as I am. I'll let them know you declined the offer."

"Wait, hold on," I said quickly, my mind still reeling. "I never said I declined. But... you'd actually let me go stay with them?"

He closed his eyes for a moment, exhaling deeply, as though steeling himself. "This goes against everything I've done to keep you safe and under my watch." His voice was steady, but there was something different in the way he spoke—more controlled, almost like he was talking himself into something.

He took another measured breath, then looked back at me. "But there was something in your eyes that made me think twice about it."

If I didn't know any better, I'd say he almost looked... defeated. The man who had always been so steadfast, so unshakable, was showing cracks. I wished I could capture this moment. And I needed to remember this look I apparently had—just in case I ever needed to use it again. To

154

think he'd actually consider letting me leave. And to stay with someone else, no less.

"If you're interested," he said, his voice softening just a little, "I can set this up. We can discuss what happens next. So, I'm asking you—do you really want to do this?"

For years, I'd felt like my world would never extend beyond walls of the Masidone mansion. But now, I was being given a chance to step outside of it. To see something new—and someone new.

Misa was supposed to be a blip, a bad interaction from years ago. But if that moment hadn't happened, I wouldn't have this opportunity now. Life's cruel way of bringing things full circle.

I remembered the bet Sano and I made all those years ago: if we ever got the chance to meet again, we'd make sure it was better than the first time. Now, I had that chance. It was risky—our first impression hadn't exactly been stellar—but maybe, after all this time, things would be different.

"I'm interested," I said, my voice steady despite the whirlwind in my chest.

Jay always said if you see a chance, take it. Don't waste your life wondering, "What if?" I could always come back from this. But I couldn't come back from never going.

Epilogue

Jay pulled up to my new place of residence. I studied the house from the passenger seat—a two-story cream-colored home with red trim, a gated fence, and another house right next to it. The whole block was lined with similar homes, each one blending seamlessly into the next. A regular neighborhood. Regular people.

My mom got a house last year, so I wasn't a stranger to neighborhoods. But this one? This was different. This was mine—at least for a while.

"Still surprised this is happening?" Jay asked, breaking my train of thought.

"Of course I am." I rolled down the window, letting the outside air fill my lungs. "You've known my father just as long as I have. How could I not be surprised he finally let me off my leash?" I exhaled, my head tilting slightly as a scent caught my attention.

"This smell—someone's cooking around here. I don't know where it's coming from, though. Could be this house, could be across the street. There are options here, Jay. Back home, there were no options. Just us. Always just us."

Jay chuckled softly. "Can't remember the last time I saw you this excited. Aren't you the least bit nervous about staying with another family?"

I shrugged, my gaze still lingering on the street. "Foreign exchange students do it. This is definitely foreign land, so I don't see the difference."

Jay shot me a look, a mix of amusement and concern. "You know that's not exactly what I meant."

I rolled the window back up, glancing over at him with a smirk. "Yeah, I know. I know you've been worried about this whole thing… I'd be lying if I said I wasn't a little anxious too. But… sitting here, I feel like a weight's been lifted. I have no idea what's going to happen once I step inside." I turned back to the house, feeling a mix of excitement and nerves. "For all I know, she might kick me out the second I walk in. But for now, I just want to take this moment in before it's gone."

Jay smirked, his usual teasing tone lightening the mood. "As long as you don't say anything like last time, no one's kicking you out. I mean, look at you—young, rich, handsome. Just how they like 'em."

I rolled my eyes, though a small smile tugged at my lips. He knew I hated when my status was my selling point.

"Not to mention you're smart, funny, and, thanks to me, a little better at talking your way out of a bad situation. So, if you start losing them, you know what to do." He winked.

"You've given me a lot more than that. Don't sell yourself short," I said with a genuine smile.

I owed him everything. It was going to be strange not living with him anymore. If I ended up in a tough spot, it would be on me to get out of it. No more relying on him once he left.

Jay chuckled softly. "I know. I was just being humble."

I leaned into his words, needing to hear it as he went on. "You better tell me everything, though. If you need anything—advice, help, or even if you just want to hear me talk—you know I'll do that all day." He gave my shoulder a playful nudge. "I'm still your appointed guardian when your parents aren't around. I'll help you anytime you need."

His expression softened, and he gave me a sincere look. "I'm also your friend. So, you better come to me about everything."

I nodded. "I'll give you a full report later tonight."

For a second, I thought Jay might actually cry. My father hadn't even looked this sad when I left. If anything, he had been his usual self—completely unreadable.

"Also, let your mother know you're here," Jay added, his voice uncharacteristically soft. "She wants to know how this goes."

I sighed. "I wish you'd waited to tell her until after I got inside. If this doesn't work out, I don't want to have to explain to her that I tried and failed."

Mom had been checking on me more lately. The last thing I wanted was to tell her that the whole plan had fallen apart.

Jay shook his head. "You know your mom can handle more than you think."

"Yeah, I know. You keep saying that, but I can't help wanting to make sure she's okay. I don't want her worrying too much about me."

"Then go on in there and let them know you've got a mom you need to keep happy." Jay grinned.

I exhaled, stealing one last glance at the house. "Alright. Misa should be here soon since school's letting out."

I pushed the car door open and stepped out, grabbing my bags. I hadn't brought much—just enough to get by, since I had no idea how this was going to turn out. I walked up to the red door and knocked. The nerves I'd been pushing down tied to claw their way up. My heartbeat picked up, each thump harder than the last. *Deep breath. Stay calm.*

The door swung open.

"Ken, you're finally here! Welcome! Come on in!" Mrs. Macky's warm smile greeted me, and her voice bubbled with energy as she gestured for me to enter. I hesitated for just a moment, then turned to wave Jay off before stepping inside.

"That was… Jayson who brought you here, right?" Mrs. Macky asked, glancing past me toward the driveway. "He could have come in. I don't want him thinking he isn't welcome. Remember, starting today, our home is your home."

Her words were warm, genuine—but I couldn't help but notice the same long brown hair I remembered Misa having. Dressed in a simple blue blouse and jeans, she didn't exude extravagance, but that wasn't what I'd expected anyway.

"I appreciate the warm welcome, Mrs. Macky. And thank you for having me." I met her gaze, hoping my sincerity came through. "I know this is a bit… unconventional, with me being here under these circumstances."

She nodded, understanding exactly what I meant.

"It is a little unusual," she admitted with a small laugh, "but I've been working at your father's company for a while now. He's so well-versed in what he does, and he's been nothing but great to me since I started. So, when he asked me about this, I couldn't say no."

Her smile deepened, softening her features. "As far as I know, Misa isn't involved with anyone. She's at that age now, just like you, and I thought this arrangement might be perfect. And I can already tell you're a good kid—there shouldn't be any issues." She gestured toward the stairs. "Now, let me show you to your room so you can get settled."

I followed her up the stairs, the distance a fraction of what I'd walk back home. The hallway wasn't nearly as long either. She stopped at the first room on the left, just off the staircase.

"I'm sure you're used to fancier things," she said, a touch sheepish, "but I hope you'll be comfortable here, even if it's just for a little while."

The room was small compared to mine—possibly even smaller than the one at my mom's house. But that didn't matter. A full bed sat neatly against the wall beneath a window, a dresser nearby, and a desk tucked into the corner. It had everything I needed.

I glanced around, then turned to Mrs. Macky with a reassuring nod. "I see nothing wrong with this room. It'll do just fine. Thank you. I'll try not to take up too much space."

"Oh, please. Don't worry about that," Mrs. Macky said with a warm smile. "If you're going to be staying here, I want you to be comfortable. Just so you know, Misa's room is right across the hall. My husband and I have our room downstairs, so hopefully, that won't make things too awkward."

"You have nothing to worry about," I assured her, trying to keep the nerves at bay. "More than anything, I'm hoping Misa and I can build a great friendship first. I'll make sure to respect her space and privacy."

She let out a soft chuckle. "I knew there was a reason I liked you instantly. Such a young gentleman. I only wish my husband, Mark, could see this—he'd realize there's nothing to worry about. But I was the only one able to take time off today, so you'll meet him later."

Her gaze softened, and her smile grew. "For now, make yourself at home. I'll give you a tour once you're settled. Misa should be home any minute, and I'll get dinner started." With that, she headed downstairs, leaving me alone with my thoughts.

Mission one: complete. I had her mother's approval, which meant I was safe here—for now. The only thing left was hoping Misa wouldn't remember what happened nearly five years ago.

Jay had spent the last few years helping me refine my people skills—especially around girls. I couldn't let him down now. I started unpacking, arranging my things in the small room. It was definitely smaller than mine back home, but I couldn't let that bother me. I was here. I was free. My father wasn't anywhere nearby.

He did make it clear—if anything went wrong, he'd pull me back without a second thought. But as long as he didn't hear anything... that wouldn't happen.

"Knock, knock," Mrs. Macky's voice floated in from the doorway, pulling me out of my thoughts. "Misa's running a little late, but I told her to come straight home. Whenever you're ready, you can come on down."

"Sure thing," I replied, keeping my tone casual. "I just need to use the restroom first."

"Oh, right!" She smiled sheepishly. "I didn't show you—it's down the hall, past Misa's room," she said, gesturing.

As I walked toward the bathroom, I glanced into Misa's room in passing. It looked... normal. Nothing too extravagant. No cluttered decorations, no excessive accessories. Jenny and Jennifer's rooms had been over-the-top—covered in trinkets, posters, and God-knows-what else. I was relieved Misa's room didn't look anything like that.

By the time I finished in the bathroom, I heard voices downstairs. Misa was home. Round two was about to begin. I stepped toward the stairs, but something in the conversation below made me freeze. From the sound of it, she wasn't prepared for this.

How did she not know? This arrangement had been decided weeks ago. She should've had time to prepare for this. This'll make things more complicated. If she had no idea I was coming, I'd have to work harder to make a good impression.

Then, her voice cut through the air.

"B-but, Mom, I already have someone I like!" A knot tightened in my stomach. I don't like the sound of this. My odds just dropped—but I couldn't let that stop me.

Then her mother's response nearly made my heart stop. "Hmm, are you talking about that Sano person?"

Sano? No way. She can't possibly mean my brother, Sano... can she? I know I'm new in town, but that's not exactly a common name...

Sano disappeared, and I haven't heard from him in years. Could he have come here? What are the odds it's the same person? I didn't have time to think it through. Backing out wasn't an option either. A new wave of anxiety rolled through me, almost taking over. I shook my head, exhaled slowly, and ran a hand through my hair. Then, I had to take a page out of Jay's book for handling this situation downstairs. I should defuse the mother-daughter fight first and go from there. This could go really well… or go horribly wrong. Let's see if my four years of training pays off.

The game begins now.

Thank you for reading *Inside the Masidone Mansion*!

Stay up to date with current and new releases by following Brandy on social media:

Instagram- brandywrites11

Don't miss the next book in the *Choices* series!

<u>*From the Choices We Made*</u>

All titles of the *Choices* series available at:

Brandywrites.com
Amazon.com

www.ingramcontent.com/pod-product-compliance
Lightning Source LLC
Chambersburg PA
CBHW050948120626
46552CB00001B/436